# The Fourth Steven

Margaret Moseley

Berkley Prime Crime, New York

THE FOURTH STEVEN

A Berkley Prime Crime Book / published by arrangement with the author

PRINTING HISTORY
Berkley Prime Crime edition / August 1998


For information address: The Berkley Publishing Group, a member of Penguin Putnam Inc., 200 Madison Avenue, New York, NY 10016,

The Penguin Putnam Inc. World Wide Web site address is http://www.penguinputnam.com

ISBN: 0-425-16406-3

Berkley Prime Crime Books are published by The Berkley Publishing Group, a member of Penguin Putnam Inc., 200 Madison Avenue, New York, NY 10016.



PRINTED IN THE UNITED STATES OF AMERICA

10 9 8 7 6 5 4 3 2 1

# The First Steven

I was huddled in the corner of the room, holding on tightly to the phone. The flashlight was still by Steven Miller, its angle lighting a far corner of the room. *Was* someone still in the house?

The sudden storm abated as quickly as it had come. The house was filled with silence, only the pleasant sounds of the rain running from the eaves of the top story reached my straining ears. I knew there was no one else in the house.

Then I realized it was *too* quiet.

Dropping the phone, I crawled across the carpet, its rough nap burning my kneecaps. When I reached Steven Miller, I touched him, his heavy shoes, limp legs and sprawled arms, then the sticky wet of his face.

I raised my hands to my face. "Oh, Steven," I whispered. "I don't know what to do for you." My hands fluttered down again, searching for him. I knew that somewhere in the depths of the big city that alarms had been sounded, help was coming, but all I could do was hunch on the floor and stroke and pat Steven Miller's shoulder, murmuring the sounds my father had used to quell my nightmares. "There, there, there. It'll be all right. Everything's all right."

***Praise for Margaret Moseley's debut novel***

## Bonita Faye

"An offbeat whodunit." —*Publishers Weekly*

"Moseley's characterizations are deep and deceptive . . . Nothing is ever as it first appears . . . Best of all this author offers a startling fresh voice and a literary original you'll want to share with friends." —*Tulsa World*

"Ms. Moseley's first novel will remind some readers of *Fried Green Tomatoes* and others of the heroine in *The Burning Bed.*" —*Dallas Morning News*

# MORE MYSTERIES FROM THE BERKLEY PUBLISHING GROUP . . .

***CAT CALIBAN MYSTERIES:*** She was married for thirty-eight years. Raised three kids. Compared to that, tracking down killers is easy . . .

*by D. B. Borton*

ONE FOR THE MONEY
THREE IS A CROWD
FIVE ALARM FIRE
TWO POINTS FOR MURDER
FOUR ELEMENTS OF MURDER
SIX FEET UNDER

***ELENA JARVIS MYSTERIES:*** There are some pretty bizarre crimes deep in the heart of Texas—and a pretty gutsy police detective who rounds up the unusual suspects . . .

*by Nancy Herndon*

ACID BATH
LETHAL STATUES
TIME BOMBS
WIDOWS' WATCH
HUNTING GAME
C.O.P OUT

***FREDDIE O'NEAL, P.I., MYSTERIES:*** You can bet that this appealing Reno private investigator will get her man . . . "A winner."—Linda Grant

*by Catherine Dain*

LAY IT ON THE LINE
WALK A CROOKED MILE
BET AGAINST THE HOUSE
DEAD MAN'S HAND
SING A SONG OF DEATH
LAMENT FOR A DEAD COWBOY
THE LUCK OF THE DRAW

***BENNI HARPER MYSTERIES:*** Meet Benni Harper—a quilter and folk-art expert with an eye for murderous designs . . .

*by Earlene Fowler*

FOOL'S PUZZLE
KANSAS TROUBLES
IRISH CHAIN
GOOSE IN THE POND
DOVE IN THE WINDOW

***HANNAH BARLOW MYSTERIES:*** For ex-cop and law student Hannah Barlow, justice isn't just a word in a textbook. Sometimes, it's a matter of life and death . . .

*by Carroll Lachnit*

MURDER IN BRIEF
A BLESSED DEATH

***PEACHES DANN MYSTERIES:*** Peaches has never had a very good memory. But she's learned to cope with it over the years . . . Fortunately, though, when it comes to murder, this absentminded amateur sleuth doesn't forgive and forget!

*by Elizabeth Daniels Squire*

WHO KILLED WHAT'S-HER-NAME?
MEMORY CAN BE MURDER
IS THERE A DEAD MAN IN THE HOUSE?
REMEMBER THE ALIBI
WHOSE DEATH IS IT, ANYWAY?

For Mary Lou and Donna

# Acknowledgments

I've never heard of a successful person who made it on their own. For my measure of achievement I credit the family, friends and professionals who have bent over backwards to give me encouragement and a helping hand. Their names are etched on my heart, but here are a few whose names I utter every day . . . With thanks.

Always my sisters, Mary Lou and Donna. Always my daughters, Dixie and Charlotte.

And always Ronal.

Darwin and Annie hold special places. As do Cassey and all the FSLT gang.

Jake and Tom who believed in Honey and the fantastic unknown copyeditor who one day will allow me to write in ellipses.

The gang in the Writer's Club on AOL with special hugs to Bradley, Tracey and Barbara. Remember we're all in this together.

To Harlan for special help, advice and insight.

Love and thanks to Da Sistahs.

A special thank-you to the Mystery Book Stores across the nation. Long may your independent banners wave.

## HOW FAR IS IT CALLED TO THE GRAVE?

*How far is it called to the grave?*
*The child looked up from its play.*
*The grave? I have not heard of the grave.*
*It must be far away.*

*How far is it called to the grave?*
*The lover looked up with a smile.*
*How far? From the golden land of love*
*It must be many a mile.*

*He could not see that his darling*
*With the bridal flowers in her hair,*
*As he gave her the wedding token,*
*Was almost there.*

*How far is it called to the grave?*
*The mother looked up with a tear,*
*The rose in her cheek grew pale and white,*
*Her heart stood still with fear.*

*How far? O 'tis close to the hearthstone;*
*Alas for the baby feet,*
*The little bare feet that all unled,*
*Are going with step so fleet,*
*And they are almost there.*

*How far is it called to the grave?*
*It is only a life, dear friend,*
*And the longest life is short at last,*
*And soon our lives must end.*

*But there is One who arose from the grave,*
*Who ascended triumphant on high,*
*With our trust in Him, we'll know no sting,*
*Though low in the grave we lie,*
*And we're almost there*

–UNKNOWN

# The Fourth Steven

# One

I knew three Stevens.

But I'd never thought of it that way.

I mean there was Steven Miller who ran the Texaco station and worked on my car. He was about sixty, thin, with his still-black hair balding at the back and even sparser on top. Steven was my rock, every single woman should have one. I could always depend on him to either come and get me when the car broke down, or to tell me, ''Don't get back in it until I can get a wrecker for you,'' even if the car had disappointed me in the middle of freeway traffic during rush hour in a city three hundred miles away from his station.

Then there was Steven Bondesky, who kept my accounts, and who I needed like life's blood because he was the one who throughout my twenty-eight years of saying, ''Yes, I do understand numbers,'' who continually told me, ''No, Honey, you don't.'' Bondesky looked as if he were the garage owner Steven Miller really was. His beefy fingers were always as black-stained as Miller's, only with ink instead of oil.

Steven Bondesky didn't call me Honey because we were on intimate terms, but because that's my name. I've been trying to figure it out all my life. Was I that cute? Sweet as honey? What? My name is a burden, and in my darker moments, I've wondered if I wasn't important enough to be named a real name. So, when I was about eight or twelve, I named myself Lydia. Only I never told anyone.

Except my other Steven.

My only friend on this earth is Steven Hyatt. We've been friends since high school, ever since the first day of our first class in radio-TV speech when Miss Mott stood up and right there in front of our freshman selves recited "Patterns" by Amy Lowell. It was to die for. And since then—since Miss Mott's chilling finish when her dramatic "Christ, what are patterns for . . ." had faded into the room—and I looked at my neighboring student across the scratched pine arms of our desks and saw the echo of my enthrallment in his eyes, we have never been apart in spirit—only in miles.

Steven Hyatt lives in Hollywood, directing movies that mean something to a loyal if bizarre and limited audience, but he's really as close as the book of poems I carry in the glove compartment of my temperamental automobile.

I never mix the Stevens. In my mind, they don't have anything in common. They are Steven Miller, Steven Bondesky, and Steven Hyatt, and when I am with one, I never think of the others.

So when the phone rang that Saturday morning and a man's voice said, "This is Steven," after I said hello, it was the first time I'd ever realized I knew more than one.

"Steven?"

The car was running, the taxes were paid, Steven Hyatt was in Australia on location, and I didn't know anyone else named Steven.

# Two

That was the beginning of Day One.

If I had owned a diary, I would have written it that way—Day One—in black ink, but I can't decide whether it would have been on the left- or right-hand side of the page. Decisions like that are one of the reasons why I don't own a diary. Also, should I have written Steven—Day One?

I am a nice person. One of the nicest anyone will ever meet. If I stumble on a curb, I apologize to the sidewalk. And I would never risk hurting the feelings of one of my Stevens by saying, "Steven who?"

So after the first "Steven?" I said, "Oh, Steven," the way it would sound it you put an extra "e" in the word. Not too strong though, just enough so that it sounded like "Oh, yes, of course, it's *you,* and how stupid of me not to recognize your voice."

"How far is it called to the grave?" Steven said.

I had been waiting for a clue and now knew it was Steven Hyatt playing our old game of Poem, Poem, Who

Has the Next Line? The reason for the distortion in his voice must be the distance it had to travel—from Sydney to Fort Worth is more miles than Steven Bondesky tells me I can number.

Organizing my mind to this thought took only a heartbeat, so there was no perceptible gap between Steven's line and my response: " 'It is only a life, dear friend.' " I'd even had time to decide which line I thought would be the most appropriate, discarding the other three possible answers for the one I thought would best fit our game.

It must have been the right rejoinder because Steven sighed and said, "Thank God, I thought I'd gotten the wrong number. Now, listen, I don't have much time. Tell them its over. Our man is dead, and no one suspects a thing. I'll be there soon, just as soon as I can catch the next train."

"Steven?" I put the question mark back in my voice. Then, never wanting to be caught wrong but smart enough to know when I was, I sighed and said, "Okay, you jerk, you win. What is that drivel? Not your latest film script, I hope?"

The voice was shaken, and it was not Steven Hyatt's. "Who are you? What number is this?"

I've been to classes on self-defense—every single woman should—and I've had hard-boiled policeman sneer at me and say, "Well, honey, if you can't stand the thought of gouging their eyes out with your thumb, you might as well take a pillow along and enjoy it." I didn't learn much at that session except that once again someone was calling me by my name and didn't know it. But I did know that rule number one was: Don't ever, ever, ever give out information to a stranger on the telephone. I knew that, but the same instinct that made me apologize to cracks in the pavement led me to obediently give Steven my number.

And then, hoping it might just still be my friend Steven, I said, ''Steven, stop it. This is Lydia.''

My caller wasn't very cool. I've had a lot of time to think about it since, and what I would have said, had I been in his situation, would have been, ''Oh, Lydia, I'm so sorry. I have dialed the wrong number. It's just a silly game I play with my friend.'' I would have understood and laughed and that would have been that, except for perhaps remembering to tell my Steven that someone else out there played games with the poems of unknown poets.

Or I would have just hung up.

This fourth Steven didn't do either of the things I would have done and wished that he had. Instead, he drew in a deep breath that strangled him so that it sounded like he was swallowing air, and said, ''Lydia? Well, Lydia, forget this conversation ever took place, or I'll come and kill you, too.'' Then he hung up.

I stood holding the receiver, listening to the neutral dial tone. I lowered the instrument and whispered, ''I'm sorry,'' before I placed it back in its cradle.

# Three

"I don't understand about the poetry."

"Oh, Peggy, the poetry doesn't matter. It's just a game. What matters is that he threatened me."

"Because you didn't know the right poem?"

I leaned over the counter, squashing the cellophane draped clothes I'd retrieved from Peggy while telling her of my morning phone call from Steven. I always told Peggy everything. She thought I had a glamorous life; traveling every day and eating out every night. And because she did, I always tried to remember little things that happened on the road to tell her when I picked up my next week's clothes on Saturdays. Because of the fourth Steven's phone call, I didn't have to make up any stories from the previous dull week. "Peggy! I had a death threat over the telephone."

"Call the police."

"What?"

"Call the police. That's what they do." Peggy's brown eyes slid across her round, smooth face to point at the thirteen-inch color TV that sat on the back counter. The set was never off, but I'd never heard any sound from it. I had decided that Peggy was a lip-reader. "Them. On the TV. When anyone gets a death threat, they call the police." Now she could relate; now she was getting into my problem. "Only it won't do any good. They won't believe you."

I was getting confused. "Which them won't believe me?"

"The cops. They'll send someone out. He'll either be tall and good-looking or short and smart. The smart acting one will help you more than the handsome one. The smart one will believe you."

Having already written the cleaning check—I'd dutifully filled out the stub for my accountant Steven Bondesky—I edged out of the shop, but Peggy was just getting warmed up. The last thing I heard her say was, "Maybe you ought to learn some real poetry . . . like 'The Night Before Christmas' or 'Mary Had a Lit—' "

I shut the glass door behind me.

Next door, I resumed my Saturday routine by ordering two fresh croissants for right now and two to go for Sunday morning. I was not going to say a word to Judy about the Steven call, but when she brought two cups of coffee to the table and pulled out a chair to join me, I couldn't resist.

To give her credit, she listened to every word, then said, "Honey, how exciting and a little dangerous." Then the petite, dark-haired owner of the French Bistro asked, "Did you do it? Did you visit that bistro in Houston for me? What was their house wine? Is the butter flavored with lemon or orange?"

"Arsenic."

"What?"

"Judy, Houston is this week."

"Oh. Well, do you like this coffee . . . Chocolate Andes? I'm thinking about serving it on Wednesdays."

By the time I reached the bookstore, my third Saturday chore, I was in no mood to talk to anyone, and thankfully, the shop was busy so I didn't have to do anything but nod to the owner. Ordinarily we'd spend a few minutes talking books, but I picked up my *New York Times* book section from the rack and left. I never need any books. My suppliers keep me stocked with all the upcoming ones—reader's copies they're called—and I had more than I could read at home right now.

Having grocery shopped two weeks before, my Saturday pattern was finished for this week, so I headed for home—after dutifully dropping off the week's expense receipts to Steven Bondesky. He didn't seem interested in the Steven phone call, either, but then Bondesky is only into numbers. His office was not far from where I did my Saturday shopping; two freeways away, but not really inconvenient. There are no cute mini-malls on Fort Worth's south side and I had been lucky several years ago to find the Riverwood one on the west side. From the small grocery to the Bistro, it had everything I needed to replenish myself for the week ahead, and since I had such few hours at home during the week, it was a blessing to take care of everything in one stop.

At home, I fixed a cup of tea and settled down in front of my marble fireplace to drink it and read about the new books in the *Times*. The trouble with having reader's copies of books is that sometimes the editors change the endings before the book is published. So I was not surprised to see a review of a book that I had particularly liked—had, in fact, cried my eyes out over its tormented, unresolved finish—read, "The warm, happy ending makes this one a must for sentimental story lovers."

Disgusted, I wanted to burn the pages in the fireplace, but since it only burns gas from ceramic logs, it was a sentimental and fruitless aspiration. Instead, I crumpled up the tabloid-sized pages and threw them up in the air. As they landed around my curled up legs, I turned to pick them up and was struck by how dark the room had become. I got up and turned on the red Fosteria lamp with the yellow shade, which gave the room a warm glow, but didn't brighten the corners or my mood.

While I was busy with my Saturday chores, I could forget about the phone call, but now, alone in the big house, with twilight falling on an overcast sky, I felt little and scared like I had when I'd hung up the phone after the strange call.

# Four

They sent the wrong cop. Silas Sampson was tall, blond, and very handsome.

"No, ma'am, I mean your real name."

"Honey is my real name, Officer."

"Honey? Huckleberry?" He laughed and then was embarrassed that he had done so. "Do you have any identification with that name on it, something that says you're a Honey Huckleberry?"

"Will my driver's license do?" I sighed. This was not a new situation for me.

Officer Sampson looked at the identification picture on the license and then at me. At five-foot-two with lots of red wild hair, I matched my photo except for the expression. But that's how I look when I have to wait two hours to have my picture taken for a driver's license.

He was satisfied and handed it back to me. Maybe that's how I looked today, too. "Tell me about this house."

"The house is a house. What about the phone call?" I said and then added, "Officer."

"It says on the report that somebody called and recited a dirty poem to you and when you recognized the caller as a . . ." he referred to his notes, "a Steven, that he threatened your life."

"Hmmm. Not exactly, sir."

"Detective Sampson."

"Detective Sampson, sir, it's a little more complicated than that. You see, I didn't recognize the voice, I recognized the poem."

"You knew the dirty poem?"

"It isn't dirty, it's just old."

"Maybe you'd better start at the beginning." Detective Silas Sampson sat his handsome self down in the green velvet chair next to the piecrust table that held the red lamp, crossed his legs, his notebook on his lap, and looked at me over imaginary half-glasses. At least that's what I saw.

"It started in high-school . . ." and I told him about Miss Mott, even strode across the thick rug, one hand flung into the open air as I recited the last line of that first poem. Dramatic, I admit, but I wanted to make sure he understood the importance of the poems to me and Steven . . . Steven Hyatt that is.

"And that's what the caller recited?"

"No, that's where it all started. Steven and I, Steven Hyatt, began to . . . well . . . meet . . . and read poetry to each other. That's when we noticed how many poems were written by 'unknown' and we decided to save him." It sounded like a crock to me. I sat down in the matching chair at the small table and glanced over at my erroneous—by Peggy's standards—policeman to see if he was following all this.

His eyes had glazed a little, but he was still with me, so I went on, easing the credibility a bit by explaining offhandedly, "We were very young, after all."

"Now, we knew there was not just one unknown poet, but it was more fun to call him . . . them . . . so. We even visualized a description of him, but I won't go into that. It's really irrelevant to the current story, unless you want to hear it?"

"No, no, I trust your judgment. You and this boy started reading these poets and . . ."

"Oh, it was much more than just reading their works, we memorized them so we would always keep them alive. And, I'll know you'll be glad, Detective Sampson, this is where the phone call comes in."

His eyes brightened. "It was Steven Hyatt who called you, but why did he threaten your life?" He wrote in his notebook, but I reached over the polished tabletop with the white Belgian lace doily and stopped his hand.

"Oh, no, that's not it at all."

He seemed impatient.

"I'll try to make this next part quick. Steven and I would call each other and play this game, a stupid one to you, I'm sure, but some people like football. Anyway, Steven . . . or I . . . whoever was calling the other . . . would start the conversation with a line from one of Unknown's poems and the other would have to quote the next line, no matter where it was in the poem. Oh, now I can see I've lost you again. I know. Shall I demonstrate?"

"By all means."

"Well, if the phone rang and I picked it up . . ." I've

always thought a demonstration should include all the angles of its purpose, so I jumped up and went to the small desk where the telephone lay and picked up the receiver. "Hello," I said into the buzzing receiver. "It is only a life, dear friend. How are you, Steven? And where are you? New York? Well, when are you coming home?" It was only when the phone began an awful racket that sounded like European police vans that I realized I had carried on too far. When the computerized woman's voice came on to tell me to dial or hang up, I hung up and turned to the detective with a sheepish grin. "Well, that's how we do it."

"I didn't get to hear what Steven had to say." I thought I detected amusement in Detective Sampson's voice, but I gave him the benefit of the doubt.

"Oh, he said, 'How far is it called to the grave?' I used that poem because that's the one the other Steven . . . the fourth Steven recited today."

"The fourth Steven. Miss Huckleberry, I've been very patient. This isn't my regular duty, you know, but when your call came in, all the black-and-whites were busy, so they asked me to check it out. I haven't done this for years, but I don't ever remember any routine investigation being as confusing as yours. Miss Huckleberry, do you drink?"

"Yes, I do, but since you're on duty, Detective Sampson, wouldn't you prefer a cup of tea?"

He did.

As I ran into the little kitchen and put the kettle on, I wondered about the investigation myself. I don't watch as much television as Peggy, but when I do, I even listen to it, and this wasn't going like any police show I'd ever seen. The detective seemed okay, so I decided it was me, and when I returned to the living room with a tea tray, I invited him into the dining room to be served. I poured the tea into the English teacups and offered him cookies from the blue tin. "Now, Detective Sampson, I don't think this is going very well. Suppose I shut up and you just ask me questions?"

He didn't answer because he was too busy looking around the dining room, which really was another big addition to the living room when the twelve-foot sliding doors were open as they were this evening. I followed his gaze, but didn't see anything unusual in the massive oak table or matching side cabinet on the right side of the room. He looked over my shoulder at the piano behind me. He shifted in the oak-armed dining chair and asked me as he jerked his thumb toward the instrument, "Do you play?"

"No. My mother did. She's dead. And my father died the next day after she did."

"I'm sorry."

"Thank you. It was years ago. I was eighteen."

"Was it an accident?"

"No, they were old, were old when I was born, and one day they just died. Or rather two days. One right after the other. We had only returned from the funeral parlor when my father sat down in that very chair you're in and he said, 'Honey, I'm too old and too tired to go on without your mother. I should have stayed at the funeral parlor with her so you wouldn't have to bring strangers into the house again when they come to get me. I'm sorry to have to put you through this alone.' And then he put his head on the table and died."

Detective Sampson snapped his head back from looking at the crystal chandelier and stared into my eyes. His were blue, of course. He didn't shift in the chair where my father had died as some might do, but kept his gaze steady and asked, "And you've been alone since then? In this house?"

"Yes, but it was all right. You see, they were so old that they always knew they would die long before I was grown, so every day they told me I would be alone someday and when that day came, it was not strange to me. I had been prepared for it since the day I was born. More tea, Detective Sampson?"

The poor man hadn't realized he had drunk the first. I poured him another cupful from the pot, kept warm by the cheerful cozy with which I had covered it in the kitchen.

"What did your father do for a living?"

"I'm sorry, I'm not sure I know the answer to that one. My father was retired long before I was born. He just lived in this house and kept me and my mother safe. And the roses. If it were light, I would show you his roses."

"And you stayed here? I mean here in this house? Ever since . . . ?"

"Yes and no. The house was paid for—had been for years—and there was a little money for awhile. So I went to college. TCJC as a matter of fact—south campus—then TCU. The money ran out about the same time I received my degree in English. Is this helping the investigation, Detective Sampson?"

When he said it was, I went on to tell him about going to work in the bookstore, then becoming a sales representative for first one publishing house and then how I'd added several other respectable ones to my list. How often I traveled and where.

It was only after even the tea cozy couldn't keep the pot warm any longer and after I'd offered and he'd accepted a small glass of sherry that he brought the subject back to the phone call. By that time, I'd begun to think I was silly to have been so nervous about it, but Detective Sampson—or Silas, as he eventually asked me to call him—was serious as I finally told him the message Steven had given me.

"And you'd never heard his voice before? You're sure he wasn't one of the three Stevens?" By this time he knew all about Miller, Bondesky, and Hyatt.

"I've told you I didn't."

"You're positive it wasn't Hyatt?"

"Yes."

"But you haven't called him to make sure?"

Of course, that's what I could do. I smiled at Silas to let him know how smart I thought he was. So, that's what policemen were for!

I went to the phone and asked the operator to put me through to Sydney. I even knew which hotel Steven was staying in. It was so simple that I was smiling and carefree with the hotel clerk until he told me that Steven had left four days before for the outback. I didn't really want a lesson in Australian geography, but the clerk explained that the whole film company was on location in an aboriginal reserve and Steven couldn't possibly have called me because there were no phones there—only relay systems between ham radio operators. But if it were an emergency, they would try to get in touch with him, although it might take several days.

When I hung up the phone, I turned to find Silas standing beside me. "I heard," he said. "Honey, I'll do what investigating I can do, but there's not much to go on. Frankly, I don't think you're in any danger. Sounds like a crackpot to me."

Of course we were on a first-name basis by then. I had politely asked him to call me by my first name and he had given me permission to do likewise. I liked the way he said my name. Most men can't handle it and get too friendly too fast. Or treat you like a pet.

"I guess I'd better get going."

"I'm sorry it took so long—for nothing—Silas."

We stood in the dark paneled entrance foyer and he looked up at the dining room's matching, but more slender chandelier that hung down from the second-floor stairwell. The house seemed to fascinate him. He told me to keep my doors locked and that he'd call me, but it would probably be Monday.

"No, I go on the road Monday. I'm a salesman, remember? I'll call you, though." And I held his card and looked at it long after I heard his car drive away. I could hear it for blocks. It's easy to hear sounds in my neighborhood. Especially when my house is the only one left, its three stories standing like an island of green and white in the middle of the brick-and-glass medical complexes that surround it.

I wondered how it had looked to Silas and how I'd looked. He'd certainly stayed long enough—had assured me that he was, in fact, off duty when he'd taken the sherry. I liked him. He'd made me feel safe, and I wasn't the least bit scared when I went upstairs to bed. I'd almost forgotten why he had come in the first place. It was nice having company. Except for an occasional visit from Steven Hyatt, Silas Sampson was the first visitor I could ever remember being in the house, and the last strangers that had crossed the threshold were the ambulance drivers who had picked up first my mother and then my father.

I ought to entertain more often.

# Five

The next day dawned bright and clear, a real Texas spring morning.

It was an uneventful day, full only of my regular Sunday indulgences: croissants in bed, reading every word of the *Star-Telegram*, enjoying a new unpublished book from my client list, and a long nap.

It was almost four in the afternoon, and although we call it spring, I could see the lengthening shadows of the still-short day outside as they began to fall across the eye clinic next door. It was time I entered the war room.

With the tie of my thick terry robe trailing the floor, I went into my father's room, claimed and renamed by me when, several years after his death, I decided to get organized. There on the sides by the knotty-pine walls and in the middle of the room were large racks of clothes, protected from dust by the sanitized cleaning bags that cloaked them in individual clusters.

All I had to do was collect a shrouded bag with the tag, Spring—Second Week. And from the pigeonhole box on a small, flat desk, I picked up a typed itinerary that read the same.

Returning to my front bedroom, I placed the whole bundle in the carryall hanging on the closet door.

I briefly studied the itinerary—really only noting my first stop—to give me an idea of the next day's route before I stuffed it into my already stuffed briefcase.

A warm bath, shampoo, and manicure completed Sunday for me, and I tried to get to sleep early. However, I knew before I started—my mind on tomorrow's schedule—that it would be impossible, and after about forty minutes, I switched on the bedside lamp and reached for the paperback I had ready.

It was the trashy kind. One of those with exposed breasts and thighs on its pink, gold, and green cover. I had them by the dozens under the bed, a perk from one of the lines I carried. Or rather one of their subsidiaries. I couldn't blame the publishing house; it was hard to stay alive in the competitive publishing business, and they had started their Fire series to bolster their legitimate but less profitable compilation of environmental issue publications.

This night's offering was *Down Under*, and I had chosen it because I thought I might learn something about Steven Hyatt's obsession with Australia. It was set in that faraway country, but the author's idea of what was Down Under and mine were worlds apart. I was just at the page where Prusilla's legs were being forced apart by her too-handsome-to-be-true would-be lover who didn't understand her real story—when the phone rang.

Caught up as I was in Prusilla's dilemma, I was sharing some of her forbidden yearning when I answered the ring. Breathless and a little flushed, I said "Hello," while my eyes raced to the next line.

"Lydia? Are you there? Lydia?"

Wrenched from the throes of a nineteenth-century passion to the recognition of the voice on the phone, my blood ran cold. It was the fourth Steven and all the passion of ten Prusillas couldn't stop the chill that shook me from head to toe.

It hadn't been a dream. It hadn't been my imagination, overactive and easily stimulated by too many Fire publications. Steven was as real as the old-fashioned black receiver that I held in my hand.

I didn't want to talk to him. But—from somewhere in my mind—I decided that maybe if I did, I'd find out what was going on.

"Yes?"

Relief in the voice. "Oh, Lydia. I thought maybe I had misdialed again."

"No, this is me. Are you still going to kill me?"

"No, no. That's why I called back. It was only a joke . . . and I'm sorry that you were inadvertently involved."

"A joke?"

"Well, yes. I'm more than a little embarrassed, but I was worried that you might misunderstand. Don't see how you could keep from it, really. And I wanted to straighten out the misunderstanding."

"How did you know about the poem?"

"I told you it was a joke . . . a game I play with a friend of mine. I misdialed, that's all. It was a joke that turned sour, I'm afraid. Will you forget it, please, Lydia? And accept my apology?"

What Steven was saying now was what I wished he had said yesterday. Why didn't I believe him today?

"Yes, of course, I understand." I said it, but I didn't mean it.

And he knew it. Steven tried to convince me again. His voice was low, calm, and without any recognizable accent. "It's was all a mistake. You won't do anything rash, will you, Lydia? Like call the police?"

"Oh, no. I understand now. It was all a mistake. Where are you, Steven?"

"That's what I wanted to ask you. All I have is your phone number. I know it sounds strange, but maybe we could meet. Get together and discuss dead poets or have a drink and share a laugh over this."

"No. That's not necessary. I understand it all now, so thank you for calling to clear it up. I must admit it gave me quite a turn, but it's all right now." I was desperate to get off the phone with him, but afraid to just hang up.

"You really do believe me, don't you, Lydia? I didn't kill . . . not anyone. Lydia?"

Steven's voice was as strained as mine.

"Yes, I believe you. Thank you again for calling. I'm hanging up now." But I didn't, and in the silence that followed, I heard the undeniable racket of a train pulling into a station, its creaking wheels and screech of brakes unlike and unimitated by any other sound on earth.

When he'd called yesterday, Steven had said, before the threat and after he'd claimed to have killed, that he was going to take a train out of there. The train part was true; maybe the killing and the threat were, too.

"Are you still there, Lydia?" Steven's voice was soothing, as if he was talking to a frightened child.

I gently hung up the phone on my strange caller.

Prusilla and her blatant desires were forgotten as I

turned off the light, and this time, it wasn't the thought of tomorrow's business that left me sleepless; it was the thought that if I had made the connection with the train and the previous conversation, then Steven, standing somewhere near the track of the loud clatter of an arriving train, had also.

I finally went to sleep after I had convinced myself that I was in no immediate danger. He didn't know where I lived. He couldn't find me tonight. I remember thinking, "I wish you hadn't called, Steven. I wish you hadn't tried to make it all better."

# Six

My first stop Monday was in West where, after I had loaded up on sausage and cream cheese kolaches from the Czechoslovakian bakery on the highway, I made a stop at Pages, a small bookstore that was housed in an old filling station. It amused me to see the lengths to which booksellers would go to sell their wares. Some of my clients might as well have spread blankets under a tree and set up shop, and they would have, if they thought they could sell books and avoid the overhead.

I don't do malls and chains. They have their own buying system and, frankly, one of the reasons I kept my interest in selling came from my customers and their customers: people who like books and would rather have one in their hands than a sack of gold.

At Pages, Janie Bridges was dressed in a long blue-jean skirt with a bright plaid flannel shirt over her T-shirt that had a dagger dripping blood under the words I Love a Good Murder. Janie's stock reflected her own taste in books, and the racks were full of paperback mysteries whose covers in recent years had become almost as garish as Fire's. She sold other books, even Fire's, but you had to hunt to find them among the Chandlers, Thomases and Jameses.

I tore open the sack the kolaches were in, and Janie brought out the coffee. Over this satisfying, cholesterol-laden breakfast, we caught up on what had happened in our lives for the last two months. I used to make only quarterly calls on clients, but a few years ago, I had started servicing them in between the big four catalogue seasons. This trip we would once again go over the summer line to see if Janie had any new orders in mind.

Today, as Janie droned on in her matter-of-fact way about how slow business had been since Christmas, I nodded and frowned, but my mind was on last night's call. Making what I thought were appropriate noises, I mentally reviewed what I had done since awakening. I had changed the message on the answering machine, not saying I was Honey Huckleberry or even Lydia; only two Stevens knew me by that name, anyway, and one I knew was far away and the other one I hoped was. I couldn't think of an appropriate message, so finally, after erasing several attempts, I just left the number. Steven X knew that, anyway.

Then I had stopped by Steven Miller's for a last-minute check on my old reliable Chevy. We shared a cup of coffee, my first of the day, and he'd gone on about rising fuel prices. I didn't know what he was griping about, I was the one paying the bill, but his main gripe was that if "something doesn't happen soon" people would start being serious about alternate fuel. And where would that leave honest folks like him?

"I'm telling you, Honey, I'm going to be left with

underground tanks of gasoline, and you're going to be driving around on alcohol fumes or some such. Look at Saudi, Kuwait, and Iraq. This is a serious problem. The oil industry has got to settle down. You read something new about it every day in the paper, but nothing gets done. Just higher and higher prices.'' The gentle man then spoke more softly but with equal conviction, ''And not just money, either. Think of the Gulf War. Sometimes we pay with blood.''

I paid Steven Miller with a credit card whose statement would be mailed directly to Steven Bondesky and carelessly said what I always said, ''Well, Steven, all I want is to get where I'm going. When my accountant tells me I can't afford to go, I'll just stay at home. In the meantime, I'm off.'' Then I stopped and walked back into the station. ''Steven, would you do me a favor? Anytime you're over by the house, would you . . .'' I stopped. What did I want him to do?

''Would you check out things?''

''What things, Honey?''

''Oh, if anything looks unusual. You know.''

When the doctors had built their complex around my house, after they had gotten over being mad at me for not selling my lot, I had introduced them to Steven Miller, and he'd started an account to take care of the clinic's vehicles. He was at their offices several times a week, picking up or delivering their assorted cars and vans.

''I always check out your house, Honey. I thought you knew that.''

No. I hadn't. I just breezed through my life more intent on keeping to my schedule than to what was going on around me. Now it seems that Steven Miller had been a guardian angel when I hadn't known I needed one.

I was embarrassed.

"Anything special? Anything . . . wrong that I need to be looking out for?"

I was determined I wasn't going to tell another soul about the phone calls. "No, I don't know why I said that. Just seemed the right way to say good-bye today. I'll see you in two weeks." I gave the little man an impulsive hug and drove off in the early, chilled dawn where Steven Miller and I seemed to be the only ones awake.

"Then I cut off his balls and played tennis with them."

I stared at Janie with wide eyes; I hadn't heard her earlier words, but her last statement all but hit me over the head. "What! You did . . . what?"

She chuckled, satisfied with my reaction. "Just seeing if you were listening to me. Where were you, Honey? Your eyes looked a million miles away."

So much for my resolve not to tell anyone else about the threats. So I told her.

"I do love a good mystery." Janie chuckled again and rubbed her hands together. "Now, first thing we've got to do is figure out who got killed. Then we'll figure out the motive . . . then we'll—"

"Then you do believe me?"

"Of course," she said and her eyes left no doubt as to her sincerity, only surprise that I would question it. "Now, if this Steven called you on Saturday, it might have been in yesterday's paper. And if it was a big enough hit, in today's. I only have today's paper here at the shop, but you can pick up Sunday's over at the Quickie. You go get all the Sunday papers you can, and

I'll go over your list and check what I need so we can have business out of the way when you come back.''

I did what she said, but after more than an hour of skimming the Fort Worth and Dallas and Waco papers, we didn't find anything that jumped out at us.

''I have to get on, Janie, but I'll take these papers with me and look at them again before I go to bed tonight.'' I gathered up the stack and gave her a kiss on the cheek. ''Remember—fall line when I come back.''

''Yes, I know. And not even good springtime yet. And Honey, I'll be thinking about your case and all, and if I come on anything good, I'll leave a message on your machine.''

# Seven

Many hours and two stops later, I left Temple for my first overnighter of the trip, which was only a short stretch away at the Stagecoach Inn in Salado.

There had been lean pickings at Temple, my conservative customer had been reluctant to add to his order during the slow period, but I had cleaned up in Waco at Daphane's which, as far as I was concerned, was the heart of that Junior League city. From books on glass paperweights to *Birds of Africa*, pound by pound, Waco had more coffee table books than even Dallas. Sometimes when I left Daphane's I found myself wishing I owned a furniture store in Waco so I could specialize in coffee tables. Daphane's esoteric customers kept me going during the lean times and added beaucoup profit during the regular season.

I hadn't felt the least bit hypocritical putting on a light wool navy blazer and tying an expensive patterned scarf around my neck fastened with a gold circle pin before I had entered the posh chrome and glass showroom. It showed the right amount of respect for ultra chic and covered up my denim jumper and red T-shirt. And believe me, Daphane noticed. There were no greasy finger foods over her counter. First of all, there wasn't a counter, only a conversation pit, and second, she only offered sherry.

I hadn't felt the least bit tempted to share my personal death threats with Daphane. It would have seemed insignificant beside the news that her four "very best" friends were enjoying weekend partner swapping and she "hadn't known one thing about it and would never have known about it, if they hadn't had that unfortunate boating accident weekend last."

I turned into the sanctuary of the Stagecoach Inn, and was so tired I could barely nod and sign my name for the desk clerk, someone I didn't know but who was expecting me anyway.

Staring at the inviting, turned-down bed in my room, I felt my body arguing over whether it wanted sleep or food. The sleep side didn't like it, but it was a sin to visit Salado and not go to the dining room. I think there are even rules about it written on the back of the door. At least the hours they served. Walking across the decked walk to the famous eatery, I remembered, as I did every time I stopped there, how embarrassed I had been the first time I visited. I knew there was a renowned restaurant at the Stagecoach Inn, but naturally I figured it was in the Inn. Only after the coffee shop waitress had looked shocked that I was actually going to order something to eat, and a cheeseburger at that, did I find out that the dining room was outside and over a ways.

"I knew that," I told her and, "Yes, well, maybe I will go on over, after all." That had been a long time ago, when I first charted my route through South Texas, and now I just shrugged back into my blazer (sometimes people from Waco eat there) and joined the other guests for the historic restaurant's "no menu, but are you going to love this dinner."

The turkey and dressing woke me up, and my favorite waitress brought me a side order of banana fritters, which were served only for lunch, but now available to me whenever I came. All the payment she wanted for that extra service was for me to listen to her gripes about her trucker boyfriend. Since she was fifty-two years old and had lived in nearby Belton all her life, I discounted her threats to move to Austin to experience big city life, and only murmured, "Well, well, think of that," as I finished my dinner with real coffee and a strawberry kiss.

A slave to my own self-imposed routine—I don't function at all without one—I went over the day's orders before I tackled the newspapers I had lugged up to my room. I had even bought *USA Today*.

Finally, I shoved all the work papers back into my briefcase, and while I continued to towel-dry my hair, I began to once more go over the papers Janie and I had collected earlier that morning. I found a yellow legal pad in my briefcase and started a list of deaths, natural and un.

As my hair dried, bright red permed curls springing to life from beneath imprisoning moisture, the list grew. Even limiting the deaths to men over twenty-one not in the hospital or local nursing home, the number of lines on my pad grew long. Out of Texas was shorter, but as uninformative as the ones in.

What did I know about solving a murder?

About eleven o'clock, I threw the whole mess across the room and then had to get up and take a wet soapy washrag to the ink mark my pen had left when it struck the wall.

Back in bed, I said, "Murder, schumurder," and reached for good old Prusilla to put me to sleep, but not even her ultimate sacrifice settled me, so I rooted around the foot of the bed for something else and came up with the unread business portion of *USA Today*.

"Ah, ha, Steven Miller would love this one," I said aloud. It was an international story of how a formula for synthetic automotive fuel had blown up in Italy, ruining its inventor's chances for the prestigious Colgan Prize in Chemistry. The originator of the concoction had been thought to be a shoo-in, and now the explosion proved that the stuff didn't work.

I thought of Steven Miller shaking his head over the story, and then I thought of him watching my house, watching over me, and I fell asleep.

# Eight

It was only when I called my home phone the next morning and punched in the secret code that allowed me to retrieve my messages that I realized I hadn't called Detective Silas Sampson the day before. That wasn't like me; if I promised to do something, I always followed through.

Now here was Silas's voice telling me that I'd forgotten to check in with him on Monday. As the machine kept playing, he told me three times that I should call him as soon as possible, each message a little more anxious than the first.

I was put right through to him, and although he sounded upset, I thought he also sounded relieved to hear my voice. ''I was worried about you, Honey.''

I was surprised. ''Why? You had my itinerary. You knew where I'd be. Why didn't you call me?'' It sounded logical to me, but maybe not the man I still called ''Peggy's policeman'' in my mind.

Silas paused before answering, ''Oh, right. I forgot.

You're in . . ." I heard the sound of papers rustling. "In Salado. At the Stagecoach Inn."

"Right. I'm always right where I say I'll be."

"When you didn't call, I thought maybe something had happened to you. That your fourth Steven had caught up with you. That you were . . . in trouble." He finished the sentence lamely.

"Why?" I asked again. "Did you find out something? Did you find out who Steven is? Who is he?"

"Nah, nothing like that. As a matter of fact, there's been absolutely zip on everything. I ran the MO through channels. I interviewed your doctors at the clinic. They're all crazy about you, by the way. Checked homicide for murders. And nothing. Zip, like I said."

"So, Detective Sampson, what do we do now?"

"You do nothing. I'll keep an eye out here and you go ahead and follow your schedule . . . er . . . itinerary for the next two weeks. It probably was a crank call . . . some kid playing a joke. And the similarity of the poems? Just a fluke on his part."

I didn't say anything.

"Well, I'll keep on checking on it, but like I said, there isn't much to go on, and with you out of town and all, I don't reckon there'll be any danger to you if there was. By the time you get back, you'll have forgotten all about it."

I didn't say anything.

"But check in with me, or if I hear anything, I'll call you."

Pause.

"Okay, Honey? Honey? Are you there? Hello?"

I made a decision. "Yes, Silas. I'm here. I was just thinking. I want to apologize again." Actually I hadn't apologized the first time. "For not calling you yesterday. I was working very hard and, of course, you're right. If I can forget what happened in just one day, I'll surely forget it for good while I'm on the road. But thank you for all your efforts."

"I didn't do much. The computers do all the work nowadays, but I'll stay in touch. If that's all right with you?"

"Of course, I'd appreciate that." We hung up and I wondered if I'd just told him I appreciated the work he was doing for me or if I had thanked him for his apparent interest in me.

There were no other calls on my machine, so I left Saledo to work the rest of my territory. I had squashed all the newspapers into the motel dumpster before pulling out, but I kept the clipping on the alternate fuel explosion to show to Steven Miller when I got home.

I took with me a vague sense of guilt that I hadn't told Silas about the second Steven call. Why hadn't I told him? Was it because I thought he was incompetent or that I was still remembering the thrill of fear that crept over me when I had talked to Steven? Why did I feel this thing was just between Steven and me now?

Spring in the Texas hill country is like no other—no other I'd ever seen—and while that wasn't much, Texas in its seasonal glory was.

I didn't even put in a book-on-tape to "read" as I made my way through nature's garden after my turnoff at San Marcos. Instead, I tuned to a classical music station and reveled in the combination of Beethoven crescendos and eye-stopping mounds of color.

The bluebonnets had to be the queen of the bunch, but the wild buttercups and poppies were an impressive court for the blue majesties. Just when you thought you couldn't imagine a more astounding sight of color, another field would swing into view; a field of white Queen Anne's lace at the foot of an incline of bluebonnets that descended into the next field over worn, split-rail fencing into a flush of pink wine cups before rushing back to reinstate the supremacy of the state's treasured bloom.

I made my regular stops, drunk with the color and the music that filled my soul even as I filled in order blanks. And it was almost with relief that I finally began my descent into the bowels of the Texas Valley where green cotton fields and aloe vera farms relieved the strain of my always searching eyes as they obliged the signal from my brain to not miss even one isolated winecup by the side of the road.

Before I left the wildflowers behind, I wanted to stop the car and get out and wallow in the fields. I wanted to take off my shoes and feel the clover cool between my toes while the black-eyed Susans tickled my knees. I wanted to, but I didn't. I succumbed only in my imagination as I passed the miles and miles of colorful (blue-blue-blue) quiet and secret places.

Having finished my first week, I was right on schedule as the Malibu ate up the miles on the straight road that ran down, down, down. As the car and I raced toward sea level, it was as if I was not the driver in control; rather the blue hunk and I were on an elevator that took us lower, using miles instead of floors to gauge our descent.

To clear my head, I rolled down the window and crunched into the onion-laden barbecue sandwich I had picked up at Cotton's when I had turned off at Robstown. The warm breeze that filled the car was as full of the tantalizing aroma as my sandwich, which was so soggy and moist that I licked it from my fingers. I enjoyed the increasingly heavy air of the approaching Gulf as it first caressed the acres of onion fields before swirling around the curls on my forehead.

I took a swig of my real bottled Coke and put it back in the car caddy by the window. I felt so free. So carefree.

I arrived at South Padre Island at three o'clock, an hour ahead of schedule. After snaking across the Port Isabel Causeway, I came to my first stop on the island beside the median that held the statue of the old padre himself. "I'm back," I whispered to him before it was my turn to go. I swung the car onto the main drag.

Because I was early, I turned off to a side street leading to the Gulf side and parked the car on the street beside the few remaining duned accesses to the beach. I locked the car, and with only my keys in my hand, I started up and across it. Tiny, transparent crabs scuttled out of the way of my approaching footfall, back into their minature holes in the white sand where they turned and stared out, as if daring me to make a mistake in my next step. I followed the morning glory vine up the sandy hill, my sandaled feet kicking up little avalanches that held the blades of the sea oats for a minute before the hot, steady wind released them.

When I reached the top of the dune, I stopped and let the full impact of the Gulf breezes hit me in never-ending gusts. They evaporated the perspiration that had formed on my face on the upward trudge and filled the skirt of my flowered sundress before slapping the fabric against my legs. They wiped away the tears that formed at the corners of my eyes as I stared out at the sight that was always with me; waves rolling in to the shore as unceasingly as the wind that blew them to white-capped peaks. Their roar filled my head, and like every other slave to the oceans, I went down to meet them, shucking my sandals when I reached the previous high tide line that had wet and cooled the hot sand.

Never stopping, I plunged straight into the water and on about three feet before the breaking waves grabbed the bottom of my skirt. I gathered it with the hand that held the keys and raised it above my knees. "I'm back. I made it again," I shouted, feeling like Esmeralda must have when she reached Notre Dame.

# Nine

I slipped quietly into the Sandscript Bookstore, but the clear tinkle of the bell above the door announced to the proprietor that I was there. It was exactly four o'clock.

"Hi," I said shyly.

"Hi, yourself," he said.

I could see his red hair above the middle paperback rack at the front of the shop, and then I knew he was standing on tiptoe to peer over the top.

"You arrived early, I see. You've already had communion." His brown eyes indicated my sandy toes and the wet scalloped hem of my dress.

"You mean baptism," I said as I watched him navigate the racks to where I was standing.

"No, communion . . . with the sea. I'll take care of the baptism," he said, and he kissed me.

Before I let go and kissed him back, I said, "Are we alone?"

He threw his head back and laughed while he drew me into his arms, snuggling my wild curls under his chin, a good fit for both of us as he was just that much taller than me.

"Yes, we're alone."

So I kissed him then, and when he raised his head, he licked his lips, tasting the salt left by the wind and said, "Umm . . . honey," and I didn't know if he was saying my name or talking about my taste.

"Umm . . . Harry." And I kissed him again and then buried my face in his neck, his own personal smell of suntan lotion, sun, and warm skin welcoming me home as much as the lacy waves had an hour ago.

Harry sighed. "I'd be mad because you did not come here as soon as you crossed the bridge, but I know by now that it wouldn't do any good. Oh, Honey, I wish you'd trust me."

I pulled back so he could see my cocked eyebrow.

He laughed again and said, "Well, at least enough to give me credit for the sense to remember what day—and what hour—you're arriving. Honestly, now, Honey, have you ever caught me when I've not been ready for you? Or with someone else?"

Struggling out of his arms, I reached down to pick up my briefcase from where I had dropped it when I had reached to return his embrace. "Honestly, now, Harry." I mocked his indignant tone. "No, I haven't. Not since . . . well, you know."

"Not since the Marines landed, you mean?"

I blushed but grinned. "Well, you've got to admit there are fewer customers in bikinis in here today."

"There're no customers at all," but he, too, grinned at the recollection of how I had found him the first time I had added the island bookstore to my client list: sun-bronzed blondes, brunettes, and redheads draped over the counter and draped over Harry with books in one hand and cold beers in the other.

I had stood in the doorway, staring up first at the brass bell above the door and then at the indoor beach blanket bingo game I seemed to have interrupted. I must have looked like someone's lost child come in out of the sun to those body beautifuls. Harry had met my stare and said, "Hello, luv, can we help you?"

About that time, a cold wet sensation pressed against my left shin. I looked down and gasped. There stood the biggest dog I have ever seen. Yellow-brown and slobbering. On me. I'd never had a dog; Mother was allergic. But I knew you didn't own them . . . you had them. Or they had you. I told myself I wasn't scared, but I was. He was a full grown Labrador retriever with a head as as big as mine.

Harry sensed my fear. "That's Bailey. He's friendly."

Right.

"I'm your new book rep from Constant Books," I'd croaked. "Honey Huckleberry. Are you Harry Armstead? I have an appointment. This is Thursday, isn't it?" I knew it was. I never miss an appointment. I rattled on, "But if you're busy, and you seem to be, then I'll just call you after I've settled in and maybe we can get together later when you've not so busy. And can you tell your Bailey to move?"

Harry had laughed—he was always laughing—and had slapped one of the blondes on her tanned backside, his fingers sliding down her leg as if to lessen the blow and said, "Of course you are. Honey Huckleberry. Of course it is. Thursday. That's it then, girls. Party's over. Off with the lot of you." And like a bevy of wicked witches, they just melted away and I'd never seen them since, but I always thought I would. And now, with Harry and me being . . . so close, I never took that chance. I always showed up at exactly the time I said and always left the same way. Whatever Harry did when I was not there was Harry's business, and I didn't want to know anything about it.

Now I laid my briefcase on the wicker chair by the counter and said, "So, how have you been, Harry?"

He went around the counter and leaned over it, placing his chin in his hands and resting his elbows on the wood. "Can't complain, luv, and yourself?" His face was serious, but I knew that he was still grinning inside at what he called my "settling in ritual." But I couldn't help it. I just had to have a few minutes of transition before I could relax and remember that I was with Harry and it was all right for him to make me feel the way he made me feel.

Bailey helped. With a rush and a woof, he came charging out of the back room, the one where Harry kept the duplicate stock. We were old friends now. Finally. All it had really taken was for me to look, really look, into his dark eyes. I hadn't known that dogs were so intelligent. That you could actually see them thinking and making decisions. Bailey had decided I was an okay person. Okay for him. And Harry.

Harry straightened up suddenly and said, "Be a luv and give me your keys. I know you've locked your car. I'll get your bags; then I'll lock up the shop and we'll go up and have tea. It's that time, you know?"

"Yes, its four o'clock. Little after." Damn, I was still being stiff as a board, but Harry had come to expect that when I first arrived. "I'm just going to call for my messages first. You don't mind? I'll punch in my credit card number, of course.''

Harry took the keys, shook his head—we'd had this conversation before—and left to get the bags. I never could bring myself to just cart them in. That seemed so . . . I don't know . . . like I expected something or took the situation for granted . . . or . . . I don't know.

There was a message from one of my neighbor doctors who said he was worried about me since the police had come to call and one from Janie Bridges who said, ''Honey, Janie. Call me quick. The jig's up. The game's afoot.'' I glanced at my watch and decided to call Janie first before she closed Pages for the day. Bailey snuffled at my feet, licking the salty sand from my toes as I punched buttons on the phone.

''Janie? Honey. What's up?''

''Honey, I'm so excited. I've figured it out. I know where Steven is. Well, at least, I'm pretty sure I do. After she left, I thought about what she'd said and I know I'm right. I just know it.''

Steven.

I hadn't thought about him for days. Not seriously anyway. And of course not since I'd crossed over onto the island. More than an hour ago.

''What are you talking about? Who is she? And where is Steven?''

''A customer I had this afternoon. She was this nice lady who asked specifically for Cristie's *Murder on the Orient Express*. You know, the one where every character turned out to be the murderer? It was one of her favorites, and we were talking murders, and she said she loved that one because of the train. That she missed train travel in the United States. That no one does it like the

Europeans. And after she left, I got to thinking about what she'd said. And she's right, you know, that's where Steven is."

When Janie paused, not because she was finished but because she was gathering wind for her next verbal onslaught, I quickly interjected, "On a train? We know that, Janie."

"No, not just on a train. He's in Europe."

"Europe?"

"Yes. Now, think about it, Honey. Like I did. Where else does someone tell someone that they've going to catch the next train out as if that was an everyday experience or the expected mode of transportation? Or the logical choice?"

"New York, Philadelphia, Chicago."

"What?"

"Commuter trains. They have schedules, and they're the preferred method of travel if you're a commuter."

"Well, maybe, but . . ." Janie would not let go of her brilliant deduction. "Tell me, Honey, did it sound like a commuter train to you?"

Did it sound like a commuter train to me?

I closed my eyes and again heard the sound of a train pulling into a station, the screeching and groaning of steel wheels as it was braked into silent submission. In my mind's eye I saw a solitary figure clothed in a trench coat standing at a telephone booth, a hand held over one ear, the other pressed hard against a black receiver, pleading to the person on the other line. "I didn't kill anyone, Lydia. Please believe me."

Before my vision faded, I caught a glimpse of high, blackened ceilings, crisscrossed with a system of intricately webbed metal supports forming a symmetrical pattern against the higher skylights of what? A train station. A European train station. Janie was right. It felt right.

I shook my head like a dog does after being held upside down.

"Honey. Honey? Are you there?"

What was happening to me? Why was it that, every time I picked up a phone, I experienced a vision, a feeling of Steven? Where did I go into myself when I held a phone now? Why were people always asking me if I was there?

"I'm here. I'm sorry, Janie. I was thinking about what you've said. You might be right. In fact, I think you're definitely on to something. All those mysteries are paying off for you. You'll earn your Sherlock Holmes badge yet." My words sounded patronizing to my ears, but to Janie they were exactly what she wanted to hear.

"Thanks, Honey. I'll keep on thinking about the case. Steven and you and the poems. And, of course, the train."

We hung up, and as I was dialing again, I realized Harry had returned with my bags and was standing beside me. How long had he stood there? And what had he heard? Both he and Bailey had their heads cocked toward me.

"Are you almost through?"

"Yes, just one more call."

"To Steven?"

"What?"

"Honey, you were standing there muttering, 'Steven, Steven, Steven' to yourself, so I assumed you were calling someone named Steven."

"No, no," I denied. "Ralph. Dr. Ralph Ketchum.

He's one of my neighbors, and he probably won't be available, so I'll just be a minute more."

Harry put down the smaller bag to pat my shoulder. "It's all right, Honey. I didn't mean to upset you. Or was it Steven that's upset you? Remember, Honey, our arrangement works two ways. I don't know what you do when you're not with me, either." With that and with an unusual look for him, Harry picked up my bag and started up the stairs.

Ralph was in—and available—so it took an additional five minutes to assure him that I was fine, just fine, and that the police all thought it was a crank call. And not to worry. Not that my admonishment would do any good. Ralph was the nervous type who worried about everything, and I guess he had a right to. After all, he was responsible for the success of the clinic, and if he thought a real garden—his latest idea—would enhance the much-needed revenue that fed the clinic, then who was I to argue.

Bailey had chosen to stay downstairs with me, patiently waiting—like Harry—for me to finish my calls. He padded behind me, his wet nose nudging me up the wooden steps.

Harry had poured me a glass of scotch and left it on the bar. He'd taken his with him to stand on the concrete-and-wood deck that provided him with a clear view of the Gulf; the waves almost seemed as if they were going to rush into the carpeted living area. I picked up my drink and followed him outside. "Ralph's going to add to my garden. He's advertising for a full-time gardener. Seems like overkill to me for such a small area, but . . . Harry? What's wrong?"

"I just got tired waiting for you. I've been waiting all

day. I've missed you, Honey.'' This was more of an admission of caring than he'd ever expressed, and it caught both of us off guard. Harry laughed, and to cover the unusual sentiment, he added, ''And . . . we've missed our tea time.''

''Tea time''—four o'clock in his native England—was the euphemism we'd used for years, once we had discovered that our libidos were more acute at this time of day than at any other hour.

''Oh, well,'' I said as I took his drink away from him. ''Like drinking and the yardarm, I'm sure it's still four o'clock somewhere.''

This time, Harry cocked his eyebrow. ''Honey, just when I think . . . You never cease to . . . Oh, hell, let's have tea.''

Bailey smiled. That's another thing I've learned about dogs. They smile.

# Ten

Harry was my only customer who didn't care about books. When he'd wound up in South Padre eight years before, he'd been casually touring the states, recovering from an injury received while serving as an officer of Her Majesty's Navy. He'd liked Padre despite his complaints about the building boom that was under way then and had looked around for a business to buy. The retired couple who owned the bookstore were looking for the profitable way out Harry offered them, and gradually he had remodeled and changed the store so that it "pays the rent, luv, and that's all I'm looking for."

He actually lived off his disability pay from the service, and while I never noticed anything debilitating about him, he'd just grin and say they were paying him to stay away from the navy. He was about forty and a different kind of redhead than I was; his hair was dark auburn and mine, frankly, is orange, sometimes pink.

As redheaded sun worshipers, we were both aware of the disparity between our passion and our tender skins and were constantly reminding one another to slather on the number thirty-two sunscreen. We enjoyed watching the water from Harry's canopied deck, but most of our beach time was very early in the morning: long walks for me while Harry jogged back and forth. Bailey was in dog heaven, running first to walk sedately by me, then roaring off to nip Harry's heels as he ran past us.

My favorite walks were at night. Very late at night.

We'd first made love that way. Late at night when the dark Gulf's roar scared away the land-loving tourists with its age-old voice that enticed them during the day, but frightened them when the sun went down.

It was my third visit to the island, and the second time Harry had asked me have dinner with him. We'd started late, just barely had settled onto Scampi's bayside deck before the sun dipped beyond the liquid horizon, causing such an arrogant display that we spontaneously applauded its descent. Hungry and thirsty, we sat on the deck, peeling shrimp and downing scotches. I fussed at him for not knowing more about his merchandise, forgetting to be the daughter my mother raised and generally getting very drunk.

When we finally rose to go, Harry wasn't very steady himself and suggested a midnight walk along the beach to sober up. We drove over—I don't like to remember how—and had clung to one another as we wandered the deserted shoreline, Harry redeeming himself in my eyes by reciting poems—although they were silly and dirty—about the sea and the sailors who called it home. There was almost an Irish quality to his memorized laments.

And somewhere along the way, he'd called me lass. I'm not easy, but I have my moments, and that night, against the abandoned concrete foundation of an old beach house, I enjoyed one of the great ones in my life.

I'd blushed and turned away from him the next morning when I'd bumped into him while walking on the beach. I'd hid my embarrassment from him by stooping to scratch Bailey's ears. But he'd laughed in that way I loved, taken my arm, and steered me toward the spot where we'd lain the night before. There on the side of the foundation wall of the hurricane-demolished structure was written in black paint, "The few, the proud, the Marines."

"Look, Honey," he'd said proudly, "brother officers were here before us." And he'd taken me back to his place and we tried it in the daylight on his waterbed, and I'd been coming back ever since, scheduling extra days for Harry on every visit.

I thought this trip was no different, except for my secret about Steven. We enjoyed our walks, stopping to read the delicate script the sea oats endlessly scratched out on the sand, starting again with a blank slate when the wind blew away their hieroglyphics. We ran with Bailey on the beach. Laughed when the big yellow hunk chased a soaring Frisbee into the waves. We ate all our favorite foods at our favorite places: big kahunas at Blackbeard's, breakfast at Ro-Van's and nachos mariachis at Palmetto's.

I would have liked being with Harry even if we weren't . . . you know. He knew things that were interesting, like the Lord Mayors of London only serve one-year terms or why ships have round windows or that you could stand behind the falls at Niagara Falls. And he liked old movies—he watched *African Queen* with me every time I visited—and he liked to stare out at the ocean for hours at a time, not talking. He read, but only the classics. I argued to him that he might be missing a classic in the making if he didn't read some contemporary stuff, but he'd laugh and say he'd wait for the movie, and he'd reread a Balzac thing, which of course I loved, too, but not exclusively. That was all right with him. Like I said, he didn't care about books in general, just his books in particular.

I had fun with Harry. I had never had fun before—just plain fun. Bailey was my first dog, but Harry wasn't my first lover. I learned the difference between making love and just having sex. There's a very precious intimacy in being with someone you care about. From the almost smothering warmth of two bodies pressed against me at night—Bailey did like me—to an unabandoned joy in simple shared things, like watching the ubiquitous prop planes drag their colorful commercial banners behind them, sweeping back and forth along the open beach. I would squint to see their messages. Budweiser was a big believer in beach banners. Harry always said I misread them. He said they all said, "sweeter than Honey."

That trip felt the same to me, Harry checking in with Rosa to go over the day's receipts, time with Harry, time alone, but when Harry followed me to Brownsville to have lunch before I resumed my schedule, he was silent, almost morose. We were kissing good-bye in the parking lot of The Courtyard Palms before he told me what was bothering him.

"Honey, I've got to tell you, I know what we've said, but I want something more. I want you here all the time. With me." He hugged me and laughed. "Don't say anything now. I know your lag time on responses. Think about it; that's all I ask. Just think. You'd gain a dog."

His laughing mouth was in my hair, but I think he said, "I love you, lass."

I finished in Brownsville—I sell mostly Spanish translations there—and then headed for Alice, my last stop for the day, feeling the resisting pull of Harry and the tide all the way as I struggled to bring the Malibu up from the sea like a diver struggles to reach the surface. All the way, the car and the wind kept whispering to me, "Harry, Steven, Harry, Steven."

When I pulled into my motel at Alice, I knew I couldn't think about Harry anymore. Not until I resolved whatever this Steven thing was.

I'd neglected reading lately and had brought several books in from the car to help put me to sleep. It was only seven o'clock, but I was tired. What a selection; a Norton paperback of *Bleak House*, dear neglected Prusilla, and Steven Hyatt's gift of best-loved poems. I made my decision and was reaching for the book when the phone rang.

I knew who it was before I answered. It was like knowing the train station was in Europe. Some things you just know.

"Lydia?"

"How did you know where I am?"

"Did you enjoy your time on the island?"

"Steven, stop it. You frighten me."

"I don't mean to, Lydia."

"What do you want? What do you want from me? I don't know you."

"No, but you know someone who does. I did make a mistake. I did call the wrong number, but it was still your number."

"I don't understand."

"There were two numbers, but one was not in service. The working one was your number."

All day I'd felt like I was drowning, and now I knew I was. I gasped for air before I spoke again. "Okay, where did you see these numbers? Where were they?"

"You know where I found them," he said accusingly.

"No, I don't." I curled into a ball on the upper right side of the bed, pulling the bedspread over my legs to warm them in the sudden chill I felt. "I honestly don't know one thing you're talking about. Did you see the numbers in Europe?"

"How do you know about Europe?" he asked in a suspicious tone.

"I don't," I protested again. "I don't know anything. Please believe me, and leave me alone. There's been some dreadful mistake."

"Maybe so, but all I've got is you. You've got to help me."

"Help you? You've killed someone, and you're asking me to help you?"

There was such a long pause before he answered that I was tempted to ask, "Are you there?" Then he spoke in that strangled way that I had come to recognize as his way of expressing frustration. "I'm not a killer. I have never killed anyone, but, yes, there is a man who . . . died. I'm caught up in it all, but I had nothing to do with it." Desperation replaced the frustration in his voice. "I'm asking you again, please help me. Or I might die, too . . . and if you're as innocent as you say . . . maybe even you."

His words frightened me, but I couldn't miss the ring of sincerity in his tone. I believed him, but I had questions I needed to ask to quell the reservations that still quivered in my mind. "Why me, Steven?" I shivered again. It seemed so intimate to be calling him by his first name.

"Lydia, Honey, whoever you are, somehow you know more about this than you're letting on. Even if you don't, you are my only source to find out what really happened. You've got to help me." For the first time in our conversations, Steven sounded angry. "Goddamn it, you and your friends can't go on playing games like this . . . not with my life . . . not with everything I've—"

"You called me Honey," I interrupted. Harry was right, I did suffer lag time. What I had first thought had been an overfamiliarity on Steven's part, I recognized belatedly as my name.

He said, "That's your name, isn't it? Your real name?"

I wondered again: How did he know I was in Alice . . . at this motel? How did he know my name? I gasped again. "You're . . . you're in my house!"

He didn't answer.

"You son of a bitch, get out of my house!" I shouted, and for the first time in my life, I slammed the receiver down.

Panic-stricken, I snatched up the belongings I had taken into the motel. My nightgown dragged in the gray Texas dirt from the half-closed suitcase; papers stuck out of the briefcase. I threw the lot into the backseat and gunned the Chevy out of the motel drive, leaving the door to my room open, light from the room where I had thought I was safe spilling out into the night.

The rain started about Temple. If it had been light, I would have seen the clouds, but in the dark with headlights searching the road, I saw only the sudden curtain of silvery Mylar-like rain that pelted the windshield. My reaction was so violent that the car skidded on the wet asphalt highway. As I corrected the slide, I realized how tense I had been for the past few hours, letting my anger carry me over the miles without thought or reason.

Shaking, I fell behind an eighteen wheeler, following its taillights like a horse on a lead, not waking from the ensuing trance until I saw the truck's brake lights flash red, signaling a stop. I had followed my guide off the highway into the parking lot of an all-night truck stop.

The rain never stopped as I pumped gasoline into the car, visited the ladies' room, and bought canned Cokes, some cheese-and-crackers, and filled my thermos with coffee. No one paid me any attention and only a quick thought of Steven Miller flashed through my mind as I paid for the fuel with the same credit card I'd given him before I left Fort Worth almost two weeks ago.

As I slipped anonymously back into the driver's seat, I was glad I hadn't had to talk to anyone. I could have—should have—taken the time to call someone. Maybe Silas. I had allowed my fury and indignation to carry me miles before that rational thought crossed my mind. But what would I have said to Silas? That I had not told him I had received a second phone call? How would I have explained that? I hate those mystery stories where the heroine thought she could solve everything herself, that she felt empowered to face down hordes of bad guys. My life became fiction as I hit the road again and Steven—Day Twelve slipped into Steven—Day Thirteen about the time I passed a darkened Stagecoach Inn at Salado.

The anger I'd felt back in Alice slowly seeped from my heart, and I began to experience an unexplainable fear as the Chevy, responding to the pressure of my pedal foot, pushed away the raindrops that danced in the headlights.

Fear and I were old friends—not the extended heart-stopping version I'd been experiencing for the past two weeks since the first phone call—but the little eruptions of it that had kept my life in check over the years.

Fear of the third floor of our house; nightmares of waking in the middle of the night from a sweaty sleep where I had tried, tried so desperately, to reach the third floor from the second, only to wake and find my father soothing me, reminding me that the third floor could only be reached from the outside by way of the white wooden stairs that led to the gingerbread widow's walk that topped off our oddity of a home.

He'd even taken my hand one time and led me in the middle of the night up those steps, my thin nightgown providing frail armor for such a campaign, into the top floor that haunted me. That it was his office, that it was only three big rooms with file cabinets containing a couple of sofas and a rich, red-and-blue patterned Persian rug, that there was nothing there to hurt me, never mattered. The dream would come again another night and I'd wind up twisting and moaning as my dream-self frantically tried to escape from the confines of the second floor by searching for a way to the third.

The third floor and the pantry.

I'd never go in the pantry and neither would my gentle, quiet mother. We'd never told Father or even talked about it to each other. But our eyes knew. When we'd bring home the groceries from the store, we'd work together to put them away by silently opening the small door in the kitchen that led to a practical use of the space under the inside stairs.

Without words, she'd shown me how to put the cans and jars on the shelves by reaching only as far as the arm could extend—no farther; that was only three cans' length when I was younger, six now that I was grown.

And there was a smell—an odor—that came from under the steps and filled the back of the pantry. Father had murmured something about mice, admonishing us to be careful of the traps that only he set and emptied, reinforcing our unspoken dread of the storage area. We'd sometimes had incongruous meals like sauerkraut with the roast instead of peas, because once having retrieved a can, although the wrong one, nothing would induce us to risk sticking our arms back into the darkened little room.

Finally, there was the fear of doing something wrong.

I'd only been bad once.

My parents had been delighted when I'd made friends with two little boys who lived on the corner. Older, I had been their big sister, sometimes semi-baby-sitter, and always their friend. Maybe I was their leader, but I liked these little people; children were strange to me in my isolated setting.

I don't remember whose idea it had been to start collecting the toys from the nursery school down the alley, maybe mine, maybe James's or little Norman's. At first we had stuck to righteous rules; only the toys that were flung over the meshed-steel fence were ours for the picking. If they were in the alley, they were there for the taking, weren't they?

Then there was the doll that was stuck halfway out of the play yard, its arms reaching through the chain links into the alley. The doll had been begging to escape, hadn't it? I think it was Norman who'd pulled it through the opening, but I know it was me who crawled under the house to add it to the other booty in the cardboard box. The three of us never played with the toys; we only took them and hid them away. We didn't dare play with them—or even want to.

One of us, probably with the others squealing excitedly from the safety of the weed-infested alley, had finally broken the rule and slipped into the deserted playground at twilight to retrieve . . . What? A ball, a toy soldier? Then we all became twilight scavengers, scooping up everything left from the day's play.

We didn't know that it was inevitable that we would be discovered, so I was surprised one day when my father took me by my hand and led me into the backyard. "Honey, there are some toys missing from the nursery school," he said. "The headmaster called and said you and James and Norman were taking them. Is that true?"

It was a waking nightmare. I flushed and broke out into a colder sweat than I ever had when dreaming. But I led him to the hole that went under the house and scrambled through it to drag out a small cardboard box overflowing with stolen treasure.

James, Norman, and I had to take the box back to the nursery and apologize. We did it correctly and prettily, with James and I exchanging only sly looks as we performed our obeisance. Norman was too young to know that I had brought out only the smallest of the boxes. The enormity of my crime hit home when I had blindly felt around in the darkness under the porch for the loot. I realized there were three boxes crammed with ill-gotten toys.

There was no way I was going to show my father the grand scope of our crime. I knew he was too old to stoop and walk crablike into the hole to find them himself, so I softened the deed with bringing to light only the one piece of evidence. And afterward, when he'd taken me to Forest Park and I rode the merry-go-round, forcing myself to wave at him with each revolution, I'd felt guilty over the other two boxes and had cried. He'd only said, "Your mother and I never want to hear of you doing anything like that again. Now, would you like a snowcone?"

Maybe I would have felt better if I had been spanked, but neither of them ever touched me in anger, and I've never done anything wrong again in my life, so maybe his gentleness was the best punishment. Or maybe it was always thinking of the unused and neglected toys moldering away under the house, sending out a damp smell that was unpleasant and sour. Not like the smell from the pantry—not scary—but frightening in its own way.

These were the old fears that I carried with me into Fort Worth in the early dawn of that new day. They filled the car, and I welcomed their familiarity, feeling more comfortable with the known dreads than I did with the new fear that kept stabbing at me through my bemused, road-induced state of mind.

The rain let up when I entered the city limits and the freeway lights lit a liquid shimmering road all the way to the south side. It was only when I was parking the car in the clinic garage in the space reserved just for me that the skies opened again. If I had driven the last few blocks just a little faster, I would have made it to my back door before the deluge began. Instead, I had to race through stinging rain, my way lit by unearthly lightning followed by an ear-shattering blast of thunder, its pounding reaching me just as I pushed open the screen door of the back porch.

I had my key ready, but when I tried to insert it into the brass lock, the door moved away from me, swinging inward. The door was unlocked, and my slight push opened it, begging me to enter.

# Eleven

The kitchen was quiet and empty.

I creaked across the linoleum, not daring to turn on any lights, and glancing behind me at the unusually dark clinic, I realized it would be a futile gesture, anyway; the electricity seemed to be off as far as I could see. There was only darkness and the fury of the rain with occasional startling bolts of lightning to change the scene.

I used one of the flashes to orient myself and then felt my way to the kitchen table, depositing my purse and briefcase on top of the red-and-white checkered tablecloth.

There is a swinging door to the dining room, and when I inched it open, I could see some kind of light coming from the living room. I stood there holding on to the door for what seemed an eternity, but the light never moved. It was so low and fixed in just one spot that I decided it was the glow of a fire, either in my fireplace or the house was on fire.

That alarming thought gave me courage to slip on through the swinging door and creep toward the living room, the thick carpet masking my footsteps. I thought that if the house was on fire, I would run back the way I'd come in and call . . . Where from and who I'd call filled my mind as I crossed through the half-opened sliding doors between the rooms.

The light did start low and then angled up in a triangle to capture the old painting of an Italian Villa that has hung always to the right of the fireplace. When I was a child, I had liked to study that painting, trying to imagine what lay behind the one bright yellow door under the veranda of red tiles.

I traced the light from the painting back to its source, and the next explosion of lightning helped me see that it was one of those massive flashlights—heavy chrome and almost three feet long. Silently, I shuffled toward it and whimpered in the thunder that followed the lightning as I knelt down to pick up the flashlight. Without the aid of the outside illumination, I missed the end of the flashlight, and on my hands and knees, flattened my hand on the carpet, moving it in expanding circles to find it.

I touched a human hand and heard a moan at the same time.

When I screamed and pulled back, I felt something else; it was cold and wet, like the stuff in one of those buckets you have to thrust your hand into at the school Halloween carnival.

I held my wet hand up like a claw and lunged toward the big end of the flashlight, and as my hand closed around it, I heard someone say, "Lydia?"

I grasped the flashlight with both hands and raised it

to use as a weapon if I had to, but when there was no further movement or sound, I let the light drop in an unsteady arc toward the floor.

There was a man lying facedown on the floor. He was still and, something shiny and black covered the side of his face that was turned toward me. The shiny stuff was wet-looking, and it dripped over his nose and chin onto my carpet.

I slowly lowered the light and put it under the man's face. He groaned and said "Lydia" again. In the distorted disclosure of the flashlight, I recognized one of my Stevens—Steven Miller—and again I cried aloud, first without words, then, "Steven, oh, Steven. What has happened? Good god, what has happened? Steven . . . Steven?"

When I grasped his hands, they were cold and clammy. I rubbed them the best I could while still wielding the heavy light. When I laid it down beside him, angling it so that I could get a better look, he opened the only eye he could and said in a hoarse voice, "Honey?"

"Yes, Steven. Oh, yes, it's me. Honey."

"I was watching . . ." His voice faltered. ". . . watching the house."

"Don't talk, Steven. I'm going to get help."

"No," he said and one of those cold hands moved to hold me near him. "I watched the house," he repeated. "And he caught me . . . hit me when I wasn't looking."

"Oh, Steven," I cried.

"It's all right, Honey." Steven's voice was definitely weaker, and I leaned close to him as he managed to whisper. "It was all a mistake, anyway."

I knew I should be calling for help—if the phone

worked—but I was compelled to stay by Steven's side. Leaning closer to hear his voice, I thought I understood him to say, "A mistake . . . we scared each other . . . saw me first . . . asked me if I was Lydia and hit . . ."

This time Steven's voice faded out for good, and I loosed my hands from his and walked on my knees to the phone desk where with wet and shaking fingers, I dialed 911 on the still operable telephone.

"My name is Lyd . . . Honey Huckleberry," I gasped, as I told them my south side address. "There is a man on my living room floor who is dying." In the dark, I tried to see the wet, sticky hand I held before my face. "He's been shot or hit or something. He's bleeding from the head."

"All right, Honey. We're sending help. Help is on the way. Stay on the line." Then the familiar, "Are you there?"

"Yes."

"Did you see the accident happen?"

"No, I just got home."

"Are you alone in the house?"

"Yes."

"Did you see the perpetrator leave the house?"

"No."

"Could he still be in the house? Where are you?" The voice was calm and professional, but I realized that there was concern that whoever had hurt Steven Miller was still in the house, which meant they could hurt me, too.

I was huddled in the corner of the room, holding on tightly to the phone. The flashlight was still by Steven Miller, its angle lighting a far corner of the room. Was someone still in the house?

The sudden storm abated as quickly as it had come. The house was filled with silence, only the pleasant sounds of the rain running from the eaves of the top story reached my straining ears. I knew there was no one else in the house.

Then I realized it was too quiet.

Dropping the phone, I crawled across the carpet, its rough nap burning my kneecaps. When I reached Steven Miller, I touched him, his heavy shoes, limp legs, and sprawled arms, then the sticky wet of his face.

I raised my hands to my face. "Oh, Steven," I whispered. "I don't know what to do for you." My hands fluttered down again, searching for him. I knew that somewhere in the depths of the big city that alarms had been sounded, help was coming, but all I could do was hunch on the floor and stroke and pat Steven Miller's shoulder, murmuring the sounds my father had used to quell my nightmares. "There, there, there. It'll be all right. Everything's all right."

Later, I learned that the police had approached the house silently, suspecting that there was still the possibility that the perpetrator was in the house. That's why the first indication I had that they were there was when they burst into the living room, having slithered through the kitchen and dining room in their trained, crouched approach, guns drawn and held in two fists. When they reached where I was on the floor, one of them aimed his gun at me, the other at the adjoining front hall.

"Hold it right there."

How strange to be sitting on my living room floor with my hands instinctively raised in a pose of innocent surrender while a dead man lay at my side. For I knew he was dead, had known it since I'd dropped the phone and scrambled in the dark to be by his side. The police confirmed that I was the one who had called, was as much a victim as Steven Miller—almost.

They continued their military-like search up the stairs as more of them poured through the kitchen, bringing with them huge lights and a policewoman who took me by the shoulders and helped me up off the floor and out of the room into the kitchen.

More police and more lights, and then I realized the electricity was on again. I remember giving them the key to the third floor, awed at their thoroughness. A sideways glance at the pantry door standing ajar told me they'd even opened and searched that forbidding hole as a possible hiding place. I shuddered, and the woman gave me a cup of hot tea, made with my own tea bags with water heated on my stove.

She was the one who brought me a warm, wet kitchen towel to wash Steven Miller's drying blood from my hands. In the light, it wasn't black, not even red; the blood was a rusty brown, already caking and peeling from my fingers. And I must have rubbed some on my face, too, because she washed my face with the towel that smelled like the Lemon Joy I keep in the cabinet under the sink. She swabbed the stained cloth at spots on my dress and then shrugged and turned to the sink where she rinsed the towel and wrung Steven Miller's blood down the drain.

I could hear an army of them in my living room. Someone lit a cigarette, and someone else authoritatively told him to put it out. No one spoke to me except to comfort as I had tried to comfort the dead man in my living room. Then I felt the mood change as the ones clustered in the kitchen parted to let another through their protective ranks. It was Silas Sampson.

"Honey," was all he said. He gathered me in his big arms, and I cried against the fourth button on his white shirt.

# Twelve

It had been three o'clock in the morning when I had returned home. It was seven-thirty before the police finished taking their pictures and sealed their last evidence bags and took Steven Miller away.

I'd turned my head away from the scene when the policewoman had taken me to the bathroom; the only one was upstairs.

Finally alone, I had washed away the remaining bloodstains beneath my fingernails and combed my hair. Outside the bathroom, I had asked her if I could change my dress, and she'd watched while I dropped the dirty, stained, and crumpled sundress from my shoulders and dressed in a clean skirt and blouse.

I felt my fatigue as I picked up the soiled dress and shoved it into the dirty-clothes hamper. I looked at it uncomprehendingly before closing the plastic lid. Had it been just yesterday when I'd put it on at South Padre Island? Vaguely, I remembered Harry straightening one twisted pink strap before we'd left for . . . Where?

Brownsville. Was that yesterday? Or the day before?

Ignoring my guard, I stared for the first time at my bed. I choked and headed toward it, and there in a crumpled nest of pillows, bedclothes, and papers, I curled up and fell asleep at last.

Silas woke me about noon with an apology. "I'm sorry, Honey. I've let you sleep as long as I could. You've got to answer some questions now."

He'd brought me coffee and a sandwich that had its origin at one of the fast-food restaurants on Rosedale. It was ham and cheese, and I ate it greedily, sipping the hot coffee and generally becoming awake and aware of what was going on in my house.

The Steven call had taken on new proportions—increased significance—since Steven Miller's actual death, and one of the first questions Silas asked me was if I had heard from him again.

Until I answered him, I hadn't known I was going to say, "No." I don't know why I thought I had to protect the mysterious Steven. I hope the guilt of the lie didn't show on my face. I'm not a very experienced liar.

"All I know is that Steven Miller was watching my house for me while I was away," I lied. "No, he didn't say anything to me before he died. Just some groaning," I lied again. I didn't know how to explain that Steven Miller had called me by a name that I hadn't known he knew. Wrestling with that question had added spirals of doubt throughout my tormented night of restless sleep. Had I heard him correctly? Had he really called out, "Lydia"?

"When will all these people leave my house?" I asked him.

"Soon. Soon. Just a few more questions."

He was embarrassed and angry with himself that he had not been more thorough with my first complaint. And now someone had died. Maybe it was a coincidence. "Maybe not," he voiced.

There was another policewoman on duty, standing behind us as Silas interrogated me. The police could change shifts and go home, but I had to stay because it had happened to me . . . in my home.

"No." No, there was no one I wanted to call. Nowhere else I wanted to stay. Harry, I thought, then . . . "No."

Silas brought us cardboard-packaged servings of chicken-fried steak from The Paris Coffee Shop for supper, and we ate in my bedroom.

"I'll stay. I'm off duty," he offered.

Again. "No."

And he made me come downstairs with him to lock the front door. After he was gone, his footsteps reluctantly crossing the front porch, I leaned my head against the glass on the front door. I had my house back again. Without raising my head from the door, I twisted my neck to look into the living room. It didn't look like my room; tables were moved, shades were raised, and on the floor before the fireplace was a gray outline of Steven Miller's body.

I whispered Silas's earlier pessimism: "Maybe not." Maybe I'd never have my house back, like it was before the first phone call. Before Steven Miller had died in it. Before all those people had crowded into it. More than had ever entered it in my remembrance.

"Maybe not," I repeated.

I went upstairs without entering the living room. I took a bath and got into bed after first straightening out the nest I'd slept in earlier. I waited for a phone call, but it never came. Eventually, I fell asleep.

# Thirteen

By prearrangement, Silas picked me up the next morning and we went to eat some more chicken-fried steak at The Paris Coffee Shop—from their breakfast menu this time. As we sopped our biscuits in the cream gravy, Silas told me about the status of the investigation into Steven Miller's death.

"Unless we can trace the phone call you received two weeks ago—and I don't think we can . . . I'm glad I investigated that as much as I did after you called me. Unless that call was genuine, we're seriously considering that Miller was unofficially patrolling the grounds and saw something—a light or something—that caught his eye enough so that he thought it necessary to enter your house. We figure the back door was already open, and, well, the rest is obvious."

To him maybe.

Seeing my questioning look, Silas continued, "You know, the perp surprised Miller trying to surprise him, and shot him."

"So . . . Steven Miller was shot?"

"Yes, in the head . . . in the back of the head. Right above the neck. He would have died anyway, but actually . . . he bled to death."

I pushed away my plate in disgust. "If I'd gotten home sooner . . ."

"It wouldn't have mattered. Like I told you, it was a massive trauma, and he'd have died anyway. There was nothing you could have done. We'll have a full autopsy report tomorrow, but we think Miller was shot about midnight."

At midnight I had been driving through a blinding rainstorm somewhere north of Austin, driving as furiously as the rain to get home and get a stranger out of my house, and now I knew, out of my bed. For I had known when I looked at my bed the day before that I would never have left the pillows piled up against the headboard that way or the covers so scrunched up.

To the policewoman's eyes it must have looked as if I had been reading—there were papers scattered on the bed—and had gotten up and neglected to straighten the covers—make the bed—before I'd left on my sales trip. Only I had known that I never left a mess like that, especially when I was away. But to seal the conclusion in her mind that I was accustomed to such disorder, I had fallen across the disarranged pillows, pulled the rumpled spread over me, and fallen asleep, the unfamiliar smell of another body rising from the white eyelet pillowcase under my head. The uncomfortable feeling of sleeping in what felt like someone else's bed and the horrible reality of the murder of my friend had created a night's sleep that surpassed all my childhood nightmares.

". . . so I've been assigned to the case for the time being, although homicide is not ordinarily my beat." I realized Silas was still talking, pride in his voice at this unexpected assignment.

"So," he said again, "Honey, why did you come home at three in the morning? I've checked the itinerary you gave me. You weren't due in until late yesterday. I called Alice, and the motel clerk said you'd checked in there Thursday night but were gone Friday morning. She said they were concerned about you, and to tell you the bill would be charged on your credit card. What happened to make you drive all night, in a rainstorm, to get to Fort Worth?" Silas was all detective now.

"Why didn't you stay in Alice?"

More lies. But I had anticipated the questions.

Not fully understanding the rigid schedule I lived by, Silas believed me—or seemed to—when I told him that I had been too keyed up at Alice to sleep. So wide-awake, in fact, that I had gotten up and started the drive home. It hadn't been raining then. That was the truth. And then I'd been too nervous about stopping at someplace I didn't know so late, so I'd just kept on driving.

"Now I'd like you to take me home, Silas. It's Saturday, and I have to make some stops. I've been gone two weeks. I have to get to the cleaners and the grocery and . . ." Just reciting the list of my familiar Saturday schedule calmed me and seemed to reassure him as to the sincerity of my previous remarks.

He was leaving me at my front door when he warned me against leaving town.

"But, Monday . . . I have to go to—"

"Boston. I saw it on your schedule. You'll have to miss it, Honey."

It was useless to protest, and to tell the truth, I wasn't sure I was up to flying to Boston for the spring book fair. It was to be the first one I had ever attended. But it was on my schedule, and I suddenly felt lost knowing I'd have to change my plans, even if I didn't feel much like attending a three-day booksellers' convention in a city I'd never visited.

Silas was reminding me that I would want to attend Steven Miller's funeral next week, anyway, when the coroner released the body. Probably by Tuesday. That's when we heard voices coming from the backyard. Silas gestured for me to be quiet and to stay put as he slid his hand under his coat and moved off the porch toward the back of the house.

Good God, I thought, he's pulling out his gun. I followed him.

"It's okay," I shouted as Silas approached two men standing midway in the backyard. He turned and grimaced as he saw me right behind him, but he withdrew his hand from under his coat.

"Silas, this is Ralph Ketchum, Dr. Ralph Ketchum. From the clinic. Ralph, this is Detective Silas Sampson from the police department."

The two men shook hands.

"I've talked to you on the phone, Detective," Ralph said. He looked crisp and preppy, handsome in his designer suit and gleaming loafers. Ralph just killed me with his pretentiousness. He did everything to excess. Just like his plans for a garden.

"Yeah, sure. You're the doctor I called about Honey's . . . Miss Huckleberry's threatening phone call. How are you?"

Ralph looked at Silas and said, "I know about Steven

Miller. Your officers questioned me and the others at the clinic yesterday.'' He turned and spoke just to me. ''I tried to come in and talk to you, Honey, but they kept me out.'' He jerked his thumb toward Silas. There was no animosity in the gesture, but he seemed annoyed that the police hadn't recognized his importance. After all, as he often said, Ralph ran the slickest operation—cleanest clinic—in town. The best of everything was his motto, including the blond wife who occupied the passenger side of his black Porsche parked in the lot near my house.

I waved to her and then looked away, distressed and embarrassed as Silas filled Ralph in on the events of the night Steven Miller had died. As Ralph reacted to the news of how Steven had been shot and the details of the investigation, I walked toward my father's rose garden.

The stranger with Ralph moved away also, seemingly as embarrassed as I was at eavesdropping on such a sordid tale. I looked over the tallest of the bushes, a Peace variety that was responding to Thursday night's rain and today's sunshine by sending out promises of early summer blooms through new, red-tipped green leaves, and smiled at him. He smiled back, his black eyes full of sympathy and an unspoken apology at being present at such a time.

''Honey. Honey. Honey.'' Ralph was coming toward me, arms outstretched. I let myself be gathered up in them, and he patted my back helplessly. After a minute, I pulled away.

''I'm okay, Ralph.''

''Steven Miller!'' he said with genuine disbelief and grief in his voice.

''I know. I know,'' I answered, glad that someone

finally thought of the dead man as a person, not just a body on the carpet.

"It's all such a shock. Do you think his death has anything to do with your phone call?" Ralph looked at first me and then to Silas for an answer.

Silas answered for both of us. "No, Doctor, we've checked and rechecked, and there's nothing to make us think this murder is anything but what it seems; Miller interrupted a burglar and got shot for his efforts."

"My. My. My," said Ralph who seemed incapable of saying anything less than three times for emphasis. Then he twirled around and said, "Honey, forgive my manners. I was coming over to see you . . . about Miller, of course, and to introduce you to the gardener I told you I was going to hire. This is Joaquin Verde."

"Hello," I said to the man who had smiled with me a few minutes earlier. I would have shaken hands, but he ducked his head shyly and missed seeing me reach out to him. He looked like a Mexican with his dark, shaggy hair and unkempt mustache. I decided that he didn't speak English, but he surprised me by suddenly looking up and speaking to me softly with only a trace of Spanish accent.

"It is a pleasure to make your acquaintance, Miss Huckleberry. The doctor has told me much about you." He stopped, blushed, and then added, "And I am sorry for your recent bereavement."

As I was saying thank you, Ralph beamed as if he had produced a performing animal for me. "Isn't he great? He's going to do wonders for us, Honey."

"I don't know, Ralph." I turned and looked at the yard. It looked clean and neat, but certainly it didn't rate being called a garden.

After my father died and the clinic began to take shape, it was obvious that not only my strange house but also the shaggy backyard was a thorn in my new neighbor's side. As a concession to good relations with them, I had agreed to let the clinic tear down the leaning garage in exchange for a covered, locked area on their property, and for the builders to bulldoze the rest of the yard—except for my father's rose bushes. Money had seemed no object.

The architects laid out a system that pleased them: simple walks leading to a small white gazebo, planted everything in grass, and disappeared, the garden being the last of their project for the doctors. It was nothing special, but it showed more humanity than the white brick and chrome boxes they had built for the ophthalmologists. Watered and mowed by the maintenance staff, the area was a success with the patients; their children ran around the yard playing tag while they waited for their parents, and I liked the sound of their laughter. And I was home so seldom. Yes, it had been a good solution all the way around, but now, a real garden?

"What good would it do? Most of your patients can't see, anyway."

He ignored me and said, "Joaquin is an Iris specialist. The best. We have great plans. And, Honey, I have a favor to ask you. One that will benefit all of us." His gaze took in not only Joaquin and me but also Silas. "Would you consider renting your top floor to Joaquin? He doesn't have any place to stay, and I'm sure it would be a comfort to you to know—"

I turned to Silas. "Did you know about this?"

"Sure did. Doc told me yesterday." Silas bent his head toward mine and whispered, "Doc assures me he's checked this guy out and everything is A-okay. You know what I mean?''

''But . . . in my house?'' I hissed back.

''Not actually in the house. Upstairs. You know there's no way to get into your part of the house from up there.''

This had gone far enough. I turned to Joaquin, who stood there with his eyes downcast. ''Joaquin, this is nothing personal, but no one . . . no one . . . has ever stayed in the house. I don't feel comfortable renting it.''

All three of the men looked disappointed, so I added, ''At least not now. Not this minute. Let me think it over. You understand, don't you?''

Ralph and Silas didn't, but Joaquin raised his eyes and smiled again as he said, ''*Sí,* Miss Huckleberry. I understand.''

Joaquin and Ralph left, making plans for temporary lodging for the gardener in the clinic staff room, and Silas and I walked back to the front of the house.

''I thought you told me your friend Steven Hyatt sometimes stayed on the third floor.''

''That hasn't been for years, Silas. And only after his aunt died. I haven't been up there in such a long time. Can't begin to imagine what it looks like now.''

''Looks okay. I was up there myself yesterday, you know. A little musty, but good enough for a gardener, and I like the idea of someone being here with you.'' He glanced at my face and amended, ''I mean being near you . . . in case . . . you know.'' He laughed. ''I honestly think that's why Ralph wanted to hire Joaquin . . . or someone like him.'' Then, serious, he finished, ''Honey, I want to . . . but I can't . . . keep someone guarding you twenty-four hours a day.''

I have to admit I was pleased that Silas cared enough to worry about me outside the rigid guidelines his life dictated, but I was more pleased that I wouldn't be watched every minute. I'd had a taste of that over the past two days. It felt confining, claustrophobic.

There had only been a small report of Steven Miller's murder on last night's TV news and a briefer account in the morning paper; breaking and entering in this neighborhood wasn't actually news, and a killing was rated only slightly more newsworthy. But I wasn't surprised that it had caught Janie Bridges's eye; after all, murder was her business.

She sounded concerned when I heard her voice over the answering machine, and since I didn't mind talking to her, I picked up the receiver before she could hang up. I was rewarded for my efforts by a blast of feedback.

"I hate that thing," I said in way of opening the conversation.

"You had a murder in your house." It sounded as if Janie was accusing me of winning a jackpot in which she'd had her name entered.

"Yes, I guess you read about it. It was my service station operator . . . and friend, Steven Miller."

Personalizing the killing brought out Janie's warm, mothering personality that somehow meshed with her bloodthirsty side. "How terrible for you. Yes, there's a story in this morning's *Star-Telegram*. I almost died when I saw your name. Do you want me to come?" she asked consolingly before she reverted to her darker self. "Honey, does this have anything to do with the Steven phone calls?"

Janie was the only one I had told about the second

phone call. I was glad I had. I needed to talk to someone about the continued calls, and without pausing to think, I told her about the third one and the reason for my mad nocturnal race to Fort Worth. For the first time, I shared the terror of finding Steven Miller's body, the guilt over not revealing the additional phone calls, and my growing doubt that maybe Steven X wasn't innocent, after all.

"But something made you think so in the first place, Honey. What was it?" Janie persisted.

It's hard to explain intangibles. How do you say, "It was in his voice," and mean the righteous anger, the confusion, and the frustration I'd heard; that of an innocent person caught in something he didn't understand but that was so overpowering it forced him to desperate acts.

*Desperate enough to kill Steven Miller?* I wondered. If not, why hadn't he called last night to explain?

"I trust your instincts. If you thought he wasn't dangerous to you, then he's not. It's that simple. And you'll hear from him. I just know it," and I could actually feel her excited shiver over the phone. "With all the real action going on at your end, it makes my contribution look paltry."

"Why, what are you doing?" I asked aloud, but inside my question was, *Will he call again?*

"Looking for clues, of course. Reading all the newspapers. That's why I read the Fort Worth paper this morning. I was looking for murders in Europe, you remember? We did decide Steven was in Europe," Janie declared.

*You did,* I thought, remembering our last conversation from Padre. And yet, I remembered the feeling I'd had. The feeling that Janie was right on this one.

Trying to sound interested, I asked, "And what have you discovered?"

"A car-bombing in Prague. Another in Belfast. A stabbing in London, only don't count that one; the wife confessed." She went on with her list. "A laboratory explosion in Florence. How about this one . . . a train-derailment in southern—"

I interrupted, "Wait a minute. I didn't know someone was killed in that laboratory explosion in Italy." Somewhere in my briefcase or on the back floorboard of my car, there was an article I'd torn out of *USA Today*—oh, it seemed like three years ago. An article I'd saved to show Steven Miller, about alternate fuels. Maybe it was the obscure connection with the dead man. Maybe it was the surprise that I hadn't remembered a death from the explosion, but something about Janie's report clicked . . . seemed right.

Janie rattled on, "Yes, one man. I don't think they found his body at first, and then there was some trouble identifying it. The fire and all, you know. Ugh. Well, anyway, you think there might be something to it?"

"Just a feeling, that's all."

"You know how I trust your instincts. I'll find out more about it and call you back. Honey, are you really all right? I can come . . . be there in about an hour." She sounded wistful.

"No, don't do that. I was just going out to do my regular Saturday chores, and I'm already late. I'm fine, Janie." I tried to express my gratitude for her call, but I could tell she was only half-acknowledging me, her mind deep at work on a train of thought that led straight to a demolished laboratory in northern Italy

# Fourteen

The comfort I'd always derived from my Saturday routine seemed boring and insignificant today. I tossed an apologetic "car trouble" to Peggy when she clucked over my unusual lateness, and since it was so late—almost noon—I only mouthed "strawberry butter" to Judy at the Bistro as I ordered croissants. I upped my order to six; people had been dropping by unexpectedly. Judy, busy with the lunch crowd, smiled and nodded, pleased with the culinary news from Houston I'd promised her two weeks ago.

I didn't even stop at the bookstore, although I knew I'd regret not picking up the *Times* book section. But after all, it wasn't like I was going to leave town. I could come back Monday and get it; the thought of breaking my usual pattern put goose bumps on my arms and I shivered from the anxiety over the unexpected and unwelcome options in my life. Not for the first time I wondered about the structure of my life.

There was a whole week ahead of me in which only

a funeral seemed to be a specific appointment. There was the decision of whether to rent my upstairs or not. Would Steven X call? And from out of nowhere, I remembered Harry.

What to do about Harry occupied my mind as I pushed the grocery cart up and down the aisles in the most haphazard shopping trip I'd ever conducted. Just one day off my schedule, and I was throwing items like clam sauce into the basket. And I knew I was allergic to clam sauce.

I called Harry when I arrived home. I didn't tell him about Steven Miller. I think he thought the strain in my voice was due to the way we had parted in Brownsville, but he didn't press me, didn't ask for any answers. I hung up. I did love Harry. Didn't I?

I called Southwestern Bell and asked for the charges from my number to Alice last Thursday night. It came to three dollars and thirty-seven cents. I knew Steven had called from my house.

Silas Sampson called me and said it was all right to clean up the living room, that the lab had all they needed.

I wound up crying as I emptied one bucket of bloody water after another into the dirt around the rose bushes. I just couldn't pour what was left of Steven Miller down the drain.

After my second trip, Joaquin Verde took the bucket from me and said, "Let me finish up for you." And I let him. Another stranger in my house; he knelt and scrubbed the stains from the carpet with a stiff-bristled brush that we mutually agreed was to be discarded afterward along with the bucket and rags I'd given him for the unpleasant job.

The afternoon had been warm—spring days can be like that—and we opened windows in the living room and dining room to let a cross draft dry the carpet.

The long Saturday was almost over when, after walking to the door four times, I made up my mind and called to Joaquin, who was turning earth in the garden. "I've made some supper, linguini with clam sauce and a salad. Will you eat with me?"

He cleaned up first outside with the hose and then again at my kitchen sink, apologizing for the mess he was making. His big brown hands filled the tiny sink and water splashed onto the wood counter. He was still apologizing, brushing at his coveralls, as he sat down at the miniature picnic-type kitchen table to eat.

"No, don't. I'm no great shakes myself," I said looking down at my blue jeans with still damp knees from where I'd knelt earlier on the wet carpet.

I served him a huge platter of linguini and a large bowl of salad. He took oil and vinegar on his salad, and I informally handed him the bottles to pour his own proportion along with a napkin-covered basket of toasted garlic bread. He didn't eat, and I realized he was waiting for me.

"Go ahead. Eat. Don't wait for me. I'm just having salad and bread." I told him about being allergic to clam sauce and we laughed. It was the first real laugh I'd had since I'd left Harry.

Joaquin had good manners for a Mexican laborer, and while I had only been being polite and grateful for his earlier help, I suddenly was curious about this man. "Where are you from, Joaquin?"

"California."

"Ah," I said. I love Texas with its strange quirks that

range from its present politics to its earlier recorded history of independence. To me it would always stand above the rest of the states, but I knew Californians and New Yorkers had the same inherent incongruities that bonded them together as well. Like a giant triangle on the U.S. map, these states stand as anchors for the other forty-seven.

An educated Mexican yardman was only one of the anomalies California had given the world. And I'd said, "Ah," because I could now understand how Joaquin Verde could sit with his thick, black hair tied in a ponytail, his rough, blue work shirt rolled to the elbows, and huge boots taking up all the available room under my table—-and ask with an Emily Post inflection, "Would you pass the bread, please?"

"There's no dessert, but you're welcome to smoke," I indicated the pack of cigarettes that was sticking out of his shirt pocket as I cleared away the dishes. I dumped them into the sink and sat down again, handing Joaquin a saucer for an ashtray, which he pulled toward him to deposit a burnt match.

"Tell me about the irises," I said into the comfortable silence.

He told me about his love for the ancient flower, so old in fact that some experts declared that it was the original "lily of the valley" from the Bible. His black eyes flashed with enthusiasm as he told me of the hybrids and how he'd developed one of his own, back in California.

"Tell me about the roses," he said, and in return for the iris story, I told him about the rose garden. Not much to tell, really, just that it had been my father's pet project, and I thought the bushes were old.

Joaquin agreed and told me that I should go to Washington, D.C., someday—if I'd never been—and visit the White House rose garden. That there were some plants in it like mine. "The old-fashioned-ones," he called them. "From back when roses were named simple names like Peace and American Beauty."

We went out into the yard, and in the new dark, he showed me where he was going to plant the rhizomes for my garden, his design appealing to my love of patterns and colors. "You're lucky," he said. "Here in Fort Worth you have a pretty good Iris Association, and when I called them today, they became excited about your new garden. I can get you nearly every variety I want."

Changing the subject, I asked him a question that was bothering me. "Joaquin, why did you come to Texas?"

His open expression closed, and he said, "I just did, that's all."

We were sitting in the gazebo—I had never dared to sit out there at night before—drinking coffee, and when he turned his head away after answering my question, I felt alone. It was dark, and the lights from the stars above and the back porch both seemed a far and equal distance away.

I was rising to go when he turned back to me with that gentle smile I'd first noticed and asked, "Now, you tell me about your house."

His demand didn't bother me like it had when Silas had made a similar request. It felt right looking at it from the shadow of the yard to tell this man about the house, but first I told him about the other times I'd sat in the backyard at night. "There was a white wooden swing in a frame right here where the gazebo is now. My mother and father would sit in it and swing back and forth . . .

little swings . . . just enough so there was a tiny squeak, squeak sound. And I'd lie on the ground on a pallet, an old quilt that we kept just for that purpose." I sighed, remembering. "The night sounds were pretty much like they are now." We both held our breath as we listened. "No," I amended. "You didn't hear so much traffic from Rosedale this late, but the croaking things in the grass making that pitiful mating sound; that's the same."

I forgot Joaquin was sitting beside me, nursing the last of his coffee, as I went on telling myself a familiar bedtime story. "We'd look at the stars and sing . . . every song the three of us knew . . . you know, hymns, military songs, lullabies. Songs my mother remembered from her childhood and taught me. I reckon we sounded strange together, caterwauling to the night, but about every three or four songs, we'd hit on a perfect harmony for a line or two. When that happened, it sounded like bliss come to life."

I didn't know if Joaquin was interested in this or not, but I went on telling the story to myself. "And then, when the dew fell and the quilt was damp and all the world smelled like wet grass, I knew it was almost time to go in, and I'd fall asleep like a rock." I smiled at Joaquin as I finished my tale. "My father always said, 'Get up, little one, or I'll have to carry you to bed.' And my mother always hurried to say, 'Now, Joseph, you know you can't carry a big girl like Honey. Get up, Honey, it's time to go in. That's a good girl.' "

We were quiet, listening to the night sounds that had more meaning for both of us than they had a few minutes earlier. Then, like a continuation of a story, I told him about the house. "It's been in the family for probably a hundred years. Ever since it was built. My great-grandfather built it; he was a cotton buyer from England. His daughters, my father's maiden aunts, lived here until they died. They loved my father, their only brother's only child, but when he wanted to move in with them—to take care of them as much as to have a place to live—they insisted on building that weird third story.'' I looked at Joaquin with a gleam in my eye. ''A man couldn't sleep in the house, you know.''

He laughed, appreciating the story. ''Of course not,'' he said.

''They all three died before the addition was finished, so it was only used for my father's office. Unofficially, of course; he was retired by that time.''

''How old were you then?''

''I wasn't born,'' I said, and then told him, as I had told Silas, about how old my parents had been when I was born. How unexpected I was. How cherished. How protected. I finished the tale with my father's death. We sighed and smiled at the silly sentimentalism of it all. ''Yes, my father loved this house.'' I remembered something I hadn't told Silas about my father's death. ''Right before he put his head down on the dining room table and died, Father said, 'Honey, the house will take care of you.' ''

''What do you think that meant?''

''I don't know. I think he meant to say, 'You take care of the house,' but I like to think that he was telling me that the house would take care of me. That's part of why I couldn't sell it when Ralph approached me about it. But mainly, it's because I love it, too.''

I took his empty coffee cup, told him good night, and went into the house, feeling its warmth reach out to me more tonight than I had since I had come home.

# Fifteen

That was Saturday.

On Sunday, as I was cleaning and airing the war room—maybe a week off to sort out things wasn't so bad after all—I caught a glimpse of Joaquin working in the garden. He straightened up as I called out of the open window, "It's Sunday. Don't you ever rest?"

Even from the upstairs window, I could tell he was laughing as he searched the windows for me. I flashed my dustcloth in front of the screen so he could see me from below. He waved and yelled back, "Tell the nurseries. They're open today, and I couldn't wait to get started."

"I'll be down in a little while with some iced tea," I answered.

He waved again and bent back to his task of unloading something from a wheelbarrow.

Before I could finish my dusting and follow through on my promise, I heard him talking to someone, and I once again looked out the window. Silas was standing there, his sport coat thrown over his shoulder and held idly with one finger, while he talked to Joaquin. They seemed relaxed together, smiling and gesturing at first the garden and then at the house.

They were both about the same size, tall and comfortable with their bigness. There was a certain grace about the way they moved, a lyrical quality to their actions that I realized I appreciated as I finally closed the huge stained pine doors of the closet. You just had to feel safe with them around.

Joaquin demurred when I asked him in and drank the huge glass of iced tea from the back steps, but Silas came inside to drink his. "That Joaquin is something else, isn't he?"

"Yes, I like him," I said as I hurried out to give Joaquin a second glass.

"Does that mean that you've changed your mind about letting him stay upstairs?" Silas asked when I came back to the kitchen.

"No, it just means that he seems to be a good man, and he is definitely a hard worker. I reckon flowers will be blooming tomorrow morning in appreciation of his efforts, if nothing else."

"But you don't trust him as a roomer?"

I sat across from him at the small table, his black loafers taking up the same room under it that Joaquin's boots had the night before. There was barely room for my small tennis shoes, but I was determined I was going to face him while I talked.

My finger caught the drops of moisture that blossomed on the side of my drink and I played with them, rubbing the wetness around the glass while I searched for the right words. "Silas . . . this is going to sound silly, but I have to say it. It's not Joaquin. He does seem to be a nice man . . . a respectable person. Certainly competent. Ralph was lucky to find him, but . . . Silas, I'm not used to all this. I've been alone for so long, but it isn't even that."

His blue eyes told me I had his interest, but that as I feared, I wasn't making much sense.

I tried again.

"Everything I do—everything I've done the past ten years—has been on a schedule . . . for a reason . . . and this disruption—the phone call, Steven Miller's death, strangers in my house and in my yard . . ." I pointed to him at my table and then to Joaquin in the garden. "It's not that I'm not grateful; it's that it's too much. None of it seems real. It's not my life. It's more like one of the books I sell, and it's not my story."

Silas gently caught my hand and wiped the moisture from my fingers with his. "I'm real," he said.

I jumped up and ran to the sink. He stood up and followed me. I didn't know what to do. I could handle my relationship with Harry—he was far away and real only when I chose for him to be—but I could tell this big man in my kitchen wanted to kiss me, and I didn't think I could handle it. Oh, lord, whatever did I do to deserve such a plethora of men in my life? Some women look their whole lives for just one good man. And here I had two. Three? Was the fourth Steven good? I thought of Joaquin in the backyard. Four?

Silas surprised me by just putting one of those huge hands on my neck and rubbing it in a circular motion. "You're upset," he said. "I didn't mean to upset you." He turned away and sat down again. "I do think about you a lot . . . and not just about the murder. You're different.'' His voice changed. ''But you're right. Let's keep it business for now. I was wrong about all the reports; it'll be late tomorrow before they're all in. We might be excited over Miller's murder, but the system isn't.'' He gave a sarcastic laugh.

Whatever was between us was gone. He was Detective Sampson again, and after telling me to let him know if I changed my mind about Joaquin, he got up to leave.

I walked him outside—out the back so he could wave bye to Joaquin, and after he was gone, I stood watching the gardener put some white stuff in the loosened dirt in three of the freshly dug beds.

''Bone meal.''

''What?''

''Bone meal. Food for the irises. I'll have them planted by tomorrow.''

''And I'll guess they'll bloom the day after,'' I said, remembering my earlier joke with Silas.

Joaquin laughed. ''No, but hopefully by next year. Irises make up their own mind when it's time for them to bloom.'' He mixed more bone meal in with the soil and said, ''But this helps them make their decision.''

I was walking away when he asked, ''Miss Huckleberry?''

''Yes.''

''What do want in the other bed?'' He indicated a long, rectangular patch behind the gazebo.

''More irises?''

''No, won't balance. And besides, irises have a limited blooming period. I chose them because I like them and I know them. You need something else here. Something that will flower all spring and summer. Some kind of mix.''

"I'll think about it, Joaquin. I'm tired now." Before I turned, I added, "See you tomorrow," so he wouldn't be expecting a repeat of last night.

I had the feeling he was watching me all the way to the house.

When I had finally finished unpacking the car, I brought in the package of cheese-and-crackers I'd bought on my wild ride home Thursday night; those and a glass of milk were all I wanted for supper. I carried them up on a tray and settled in bed to eat and read the latest issue of *Publishers Weekly*, trying to regain some of the professionalism I seemed to have lost the last few days.

It was dark outside, about eighty-thirty, when the phone rang. I let it ring so long before answering that the machine kicked in before I picked up the receiver. "I'm here," I said over the sound of my own voice saying I wasn't. "Wait till this stops and I can hear you."

"Honey."

"Why didn't you call yesterday?"

"You seemed to be doing all right."

"How do you know?"

"I know."

"Well, Mr. Know-it-all, I guess you know I didn't tell the police you'd called again." Then I asked the question I'd wanted to ask for three days. "Steven, you didn't kill Steven Miller, did you?"

He just said, "No." But I believed him, or maybe I had to believe him.

"You were here," I said still accusing, wanting more.

"Yes."

"In my bed."

"Yes. I'm sorry I left a mess. I hadn't intended to. None of it worked out like I had planned it."

"What did happen?" I asked.

"I was on the phone to you. I had been reading . . . your itinerary and some other papers—"

"How dare you!" I said, angry all over again.

"Hush," he interrupted. "I'll tell you about that later. Now you need to know this. I knew from reading your schedule that you were in Alice, so I called." He paused and then said, "Well, you know how that went. After you hung up on me, I fell asleep. No apologies, I was tired. When I woke up, it was late. Later than I thought it was. It was dark outside, and unthinkingly, I turned on the light to get your number again. I was going to call you back in Alice. I wanted to tell you everything."

I couldn't resist, "About time," I said.

"No. Listen. It was raining, but I thought I heard a noise downstairs, so I turned off the light and crept to the top of the stairs. There was someone down there."

"Steven Miller," I said.

"No, he came later. I couldn't remember if the steps creaked or not, so I took off my shoes—"

"You had your shoes on in my bed?"

"Honey, are you going to listen or not?"

"I'm sorry, Steven. I'm nervous."

"Well, I was, too. I could hear someone in the dining room, so I sat down on the top stair and started scooting down the steps.

I could see it in my mind's eye. The dark, the rain with the lightning flashes. Someone creeping around my dining room, feeling their way around the table, my mother's piano. And Steven slipping down the stairs on his backside, one step at a time.

"Just as I reached the curve in the landing, I heard another sound. Someone coming in the back door."

"That was Steven Miller."

"Right. And whoever else was in the house heard him, too. Miller might have thought he was being quiet, but he wasn't. The first man went into the living room, and when Miller entered, he called out to him, but when Miller answered, 'Who the hell are you?' the other man shot him."

"Steven, what did the man say to Steven Miller?"

"Honey, that's what is so strange. I'd swear he called out, 'Lydia?' If your real name is Honey, why did you tell me it was Lydia? And how did that other man know to ask if it was Lydia? Who is Lydia?"

I ignored his question, but now I knew why Steven Miller had called out my fantasy name in the dark. "What happened after Steven Miller was shot?"

"The guy ran out of the house. Maybe he thought the shot would be heard; I can't imagine how it could have been. It was thundering, and there's no one around for blocks."

"If he'd only seen the house at night, he might not know that," I said, trying to imagine what the neighborhood would look like at night to a stranger. No one I knew would break into my house.

"Why didn't you help Steven Miller?"

"He was dead, Honey."

"No, he wasn't. He talked to me when I got home."

"He did? What did he say?"

"About what you said happened."

"I thought he was dead. I don't have much experience with dead people. He didn't seem to be breathing, and there was blood everywhere. I turned on the light."

"You might have been caught."

It was Steven's turn to be indignant. "I wouldn't have left someone I could help. I'm not the monster you seem to think I am, Honey. And what kind of a name is Honey?"

"It's my kind of a name," I said proudly and a little hurt. "Anyway, what happened then?"

"That's all. Miller was dead. Or I thought he was. Looked dead to me," he defended. "So I found my shoes and left."

"You left the light on or off?"

"On, I guess. I told you I wasn't a pro at this."

The lights were off when I had entered the house, but then all the lights in the house were out and I had been in the kitchen with the policewoman when the electricity had returned.

"Steven, I feel that I've come into a very bad movie at the end, and I can't figure out the beginning."

"So do I."

"Let's start over. Really start over this time. Who are you? And why are you in danger?"

# Sixteen

All my life, I've tried to live up to the expectations of my mother and father. Well, at least of my father; I don't remember my mother wanting me to be anything but quiet. But bless her heart, it wasn't her fault. No one ever actually told me that Mother's poor health was due to her having a baby so late in life. Maybe she'd been ill before I was born, but I don't think so.

The house was always dark; that's why the pattern in the carpets hasn't faded. The shades were kept drawn to keep the sunlight from giving Mother another migraine—one of those sick headaches where I'd tiptoe around the house or retreat to my room with a book. I'd come out only long enough to redampen the folded cloth made of an old, torn sheet that she kept on her forehead in her darkened room.

My father would sit for hours and read to her, holding the book down low in front of him so he could catch a ray of light at the bottom of her bedroom shade. I'd bring my pillow and lie on the floor and listen to his voice read the classics they both loved so much.

On good days—days Mother felt well—we'd get in the Chevrolet and drive around town. Just a few blocks. Maybe go to the grocery store. And if she really felt good, we'd drive to Forest Park and I'd ride the merry-go-round, feeling grand and waving to show everybody I had parents who cared enough about me to bring me to the park and who would wave back when the horse passed their way. Once a woman holding her little girl onto the horse next to me said, "Look quick now, there's your grandma waving at you. Wave back. What a sweet little girl you are. And so lucky to have such good grandparents." And when I realized she was talking to me, I'd followed her gaze and had seen what she was seeing: a gray-haired old couple, he holding himself straight with the aid of a cane and she stoop-shouldered and bent, but with such a sweet smile on her face as she waved her lace handkerchief at the carousel.

As the horses swung out of their sight, I'd turned in my saddle, looking back to see to whom they were waving.

When the horses stopped, I'd run back to them with tears in my eyes, and sobbing, I'd thrown my arms around them both.

"Why, Honey, what's the matter?" Father had asked.

"Too much excitement," Mother had answered. "Joseph, we'd better take this girl home."

And it had been a long time before we'd gone to the park again.

I'd tried so hard to be good, to do what I was supposed to do, and when I'd had an inclination to run or shout, I'd suppressed it while wondering if I was adopted because, if my parents were so good and gentle, why did I have this frantic need to race and be free? I felt I must really be bad to want something else, and I worked hard to discipline myself to accept and do good.

And it had worked. Even ten years after their deaths, I respected my parents and their lives, even to leaving the furniture in exactly the same positions it had occupied in their lifetimes, shades drawn tightly against the light, and the house so quiet that I only could hear the television when I was sitting close to the screen.

It was only on the road that I felt free to turn the radio up loud, roll down the windows, let the wind blow my hair, and to go barefoot in the sand. I wasn't crazy; I just knew which behavior was right for the house and which was inappropriate.

But there were changes going on. First I had let them change the yard, now the garden. My daring life away from the house was catching up to me. I even had a series of Fire novels hidden under my bed.

And all this before the first phone call.

I could understand why the mystery of the fourth Steven had found me ready and vulnerable.

And as I lay in my bed, holding the telephone and inhaling the odor of a strange man who had also lain on my bed, I listened to his story with wonder. It was so bizarre I might have been listening to my father reading a tale again to my mother. I had believed every word my father had ever said, and I believed Steven in the same way.

Maybe if my life had been different or if I were ever to live it again, I would have been or could be a great detective or fortune-teller. Why else had I torn out that story of an explosion in Italy? Why did I tell Janie that

I felt the explosion in Florence was related to the phone calls?

For they were. My fourth Steven was a scientist. No, a chemist who had invented . . . discovered—I don't know all the terminology—the formula for an alternate fuel, one that was so perfect in every way that he and it were destined for success and all its accompanying rewards.

Then his story took a sinister turn. He had been betrayed by someone. He'd arrived at the laboratory one night to find it in flames, his notes, even the computer disks consumed by the sweeping fire. Angry and in despair, he ran into the blazing room where he accosted an intruder who had obviously set the fire. He still had an acetylene torch in his hands.

The man had said, "Well, you've just written your own death warrant." He'd dropped the torch and pulled out a gun. "They told me if you were here, to kill you, too. Your luck's run out. Now you won't live to see your experiment fail. You're going to die with it."

But just at that moment, something on the counter had exploded, and a fiery liquid had painted the arsonist's face. He dropped the gun he was holding as he clawed his head, trying to stop the spreading flames. He fell to the ground, hitting his temple on the remains of the counter.

As the fire continued to surround him, Steven had only enough time to search the man's topcoat, taking from it an old piece of white folded paper before he realized the necessity of escaping.

Outside in the clear air, he wandered away from the scene, and dazed, he read the hand-scribbled note he still held in his hand. Though still reeling from the shock of the fire and the enormous loss, he'd comprehended the danger he had been in—the danger he was still in if his enemies knew he was alive.

Steven's story was so well told that I felt like I was listening to one of the popular books on tape that I played on every trip I made. I had lost a sense of reality until he called my name. "Honey, the note I found, that was where I got your number."

"My number? No, Steven."

"Yes, and the poem. Listen. I'll read it to you. 'Say: *This Is Steven.* Then say: *How Far Is it Called To The Grave?* Correct answer: *It is Only a Life, Dear Friend.* If correct answer is given, report the status of the negotiations. Hang up. Your job is finished. Collect as usual.' "

"My God," I said.

"I did as it said, and I got you on the phone. All I want to know is why, Honey?"

"And it was my phone number?" I asked incredulously.

"Well, that's the rough part. Remember I told you there were two numbers? One is almost indecipherable, but I've tried what I think is the number, and it's not in service. The other one—yours—is the legible one and the one that works. That's why I called you."

"What do you think it means?"

"I don't know. I traced the number through the area code after I called you the second time. It was easy really."

I said, "From the train station?"

"Yes, in Florence. I . . . I ran away. The first reports I heard about the fire said that I was the one who died. That was all right with me. I figured that would give me enough time to find out who didn't want me to succeed and why. But it took me a while to get to the States. I'd only been in Fort Worth a few days when you came home and found . . .''

''Steven Miller,'' I finished. ''What does his death have to do with all this, Steven? Is your name . . . really . . . Steven?''

''Actually, it is. It's not the name I go by, but my middle name is Stephen . . . p-h-e-n . . . not v-e-n. And, in answer to your other question, Miller was shot by someone who knows 'Lydia.' Probably sent by the same ones who want me dead. Honey, for the last time, for God's sake, tell me, who is Lydia?''

''I am, Stephen. I'm Lydia.''

# Seventeen

I didn't know what to do on Monday morning. It was hard to realize that it had only been two weeks since I'd stopped by Steven Miller's to have the car checked before I left town.

Even when I do schedule a week in Fort Worth, I plan little things throughout the week so I always have something to occupy my time. One of the things I usually include in a week off is a trip to Steven Bondesky to reconcile my bank statement, so right after a croissant and jelly, I retrieved the Malibu from the clinic garage and headed toward the west side of Fort Worth.

Bondesky's office is down behind Montgomery Ward, a small, orange brick, garagelike warehouse still bearing the water marks of the 1949 flood up near the ceiling molding. I didn't know where Bondesky lived. It never occurred to me that he didn't live in his office; he was always there—like he was that Monday morning when I dropped by unexpectedly.

There was no secretary, just the usual couple of guys

that hung around the coffeepot outside the frosted, fly-specked glass of an inner-office door. I smiled toward them, knowing I looked as out of place in the rank-smelling outer office as a daisy growing out of an oil spill, before I tapped on the glass and slipped inside Bondesky's sanctum. Those guys didn't invite any further intimacies, and I wouldn't have wanted to share them if they had.

"What are you doing here?" That's Bondesky; full of warmth and welcoming cheer. "You're supposed to be in Boston."

Everybody knows my schedule.

Bondesky looks like that character from *Dick Tracy*, the one whose name I can't remember, but whose buttons keep popping off his shirt because it's too small to fasten over his big chest and fat belly. Except that Bondesky's greasy hair was white—or would have been if it was clean—and the cartoon Bondesky's was black. And the real Bondesky was much older.

I'd inherited him and his talents from my father. "Trust Steven Bondesky, Honey," my father had always said. "He'll keep your finances well in hand. He always has mine."

"Well, I'm not in Boston. I'm here," I bellowed at Bondesky, matching his welcoming tone.

"I didn't think you'd let a little thing like a murder keep you from your appointed ways." Bondesky knows me well.

"How'd you know about the murder?"

"One of the guys read about it in the *Star-T*, and so he told me about it."

And I was thinking the stooges outside didn't know

how to talk, and here Bondesky was telling me they could read.

"If you're so worried about me," I said pointedly—he hadn't said he was worried—"you could have called."

"I figured you need me, you'll call me," he answered. He was wearing a green eyeshade to protect him from an imagined glare of the single overhead hanging bulb, its dirt-encrusted glass fixture absorbing any beam that might escape upward, resulting in Bondesky sitting in the middle of a focused if murky spotlight. Surrounded by dozens of heavy ledgers that spilled over onto two jerry-rigged card tables, their legs tied together with heavy-duty packing string, he looked like a backroom payoff hood from an old black-and-white Dick Powell movie.

The only incongruous touch to the scene was the state-of-the-art Dell P200 computer with its green, inside light displaying rows of numbers, just numbers in clusters of three to six digits each.

Bondesky followed my gaze and reached backward to turn off the monitor. Like I was going to know numbers.

"So, what do you want?"

I was used to his ill-mannered, brash approach to all things human and didn't take offense at his action or his words. If it was comfort I was seeking, I had come to the wrong place.

"Steven Miller was killed at my house," I restated what he already knew.

"Your garage man. Yeah, I know him from the bills."

"My friend," I corrected.

"Yeah, your friend. What a shock, huh? It didn't have anything to do with your squirrelly phone call, did it?"

Until he mentioned it, I'd forgotten that I had told Steven Bondesky about that first phone call the day that I'd received it. Looking back, I saw how lonely I must have been, running all over town, blabbing about a mysterious phone call, telling everyone I ran across about the unexpected excitement in my day. Now I had so many people in my life—so many strangers—that I wished I hadn't told every Tom, Dick, and Harry. No, I corrected myself. I hadn't told Harry.

I especially wished I hadn't told Steven Bondesky.

"Uh, the phone call?" I asked, stalling for thinking time.

"Yeah, the one from the guy with the same name as me; the Steven part, not Bondesky."

Since Stephen had told me how he spelled his name, he'd taken on a different personality for me. The *ph* instead of the *v* in his name had separated him from the other three Stevens in my mind and now, just as I had not once realized I knew three men by the same name, Stephen was as removed from a connection with the Stevens as if his name had been Herbert or Charley. I couldn't honestly say that I knew four Stevens anymore.

"No, his name's not the same as yours," I told Steven Bondesky truthfully.

"Oh, I thought it was. Have you heard from him again?"

"Why do you ask?"

"The guy threatened your life. I'm trying to act concerned here. Have you heard from him or not?"

His belligerence and my natural inclination to please forced me to answer in the affirmative, but I hastened to add, "But he didn't have anything to do with Steven Miller's death. I'm sure of that. But you're right; Steven

Miller's death was a shock. After all, I found him . . ." My voice broke as I remembered Thursday night.

"So I'm sorry. What's the matter? The police giving you any hassle?" he asked, his voice indicating that if they were, he'd take care of it. And he probably could have, too. Sometimes there were police cars parked outside; the uniformed officers making a strong statement in contrast with the usual raggedy men.

"The police are fine. Everything's fine. But thank you for your concern and sympathy. I'll be sure to pass it on to Steven Miller's family."

The banter had gone far enough. I wasn't afraid of Steven Bondesky. When I was younger, I liked to think that his rude indifference covered a heart of gold; that he was an old softie with a bearlike facade, but it didn't, and he wasn't. Steven Bondesky was just an old bastard who was good with numbers. He'd taken me on as a client because of some obscure understanding with my father—God knows where those two had met—and he had kept me out of some perverse sense of pride. Probably derived from the satisfaction he got from listening to his perpetual cronies' admiration of my legs, breasts, and hair. All that was crisp or curvy about me came under close scrutiny when I ran their gauntlet during my regular visits. Today's surprise appointment must have them slobbering against the glass door.

I quit the tough-girl, quick retort act and leaned over his odoriferous desk. "I do need your help, Bondesky. I need to buy a new car, and you have to help me find the money for it . . . figure out how I can pay for it."

"The old jalopy finally folded, huh?"

"No, not yet, but Steven Miller was the only one who could keep it going, and now of course . . ." My shrug finished the obvious. With Steven Miller dead, I couldn't risk driving the old reliable out on the road again.

"You gonna buy another Malibu?"

I pointed my finger at him. "Wake up and join the twentieth century, Bondesky. What I need now is a van. Make it easier to carry stuff."

"What stuff?"

"I don't know. I don't have one yet. But . . . you know . . . stuff."

He reached backward and patted the Dell. "I think the twentieth century and I get along just fine, but I didn't know about vans. Must not be important enough for me to keep up. Whatcha got in mind, Huckleberry? A Caddie?"

"Come off it. Cadillac doesn't make vans. I don't think. And you know I can't afford a Cadillac."

"Sure you can."

"Honestly, Bondesky, you keep my books. You know how I squeak by every year. If I didn't stay on the road all the time getting tax credit for my expenses, I couldn't afford to live—even with the house paid for."

"It's been ten years, Huckleberry. Don't you think it's time to drop the independent act and use some of the dough your old man left you? I think you've been stupid about it, anyway. Living in that spooky old mausoleum of a house when you coulda been enjoying the—"

"I did use Father's money. To get an education. Remember? You're getting senile, Bondesky. You're slipping. The money's gone. It's been gone for almost six years. What I earn and what you manage to keep for me through taxes is what I've got."

"Nah, I'm not talking about the bank savings account.

That was small potatoes. I'm talking about the real money he left you. You know, the big bucks.''

''Get it through your head, there's no big bucks. There's no bucks, period.'' I opened my purse and took out last week's receipts. Throwing them on the desk, I said, ''I don't know why I asked for your help, anyway. Here's last week's stuff. I didn't spend the whole night in Alice, but you'll probably have to pay the bill when you get it.'' I headed for the door.

''What kinda van you got in mind?''

''What?''

''Whatcha you want to buy? You want me to get you a deal on another Chevy? A new model?''

I stopped because I did need new transportation and knew I would be hopeless in an automobile showroom. I had put up with Bondesky these many years; I might as well stick. He'd never hurt me yet, and although he had delusions of hidden wealth somewhere in my background—probably from my father's demeanor—I was telling the truth that his expert manipulations of my meager earnings kept me in croissants and tuna fish and off the welfare line.

''I want a Plymouth Voyager.''

''Voyager, smoyager. Didn't you say I don't know from Malibu? What makes this a good choice?''

''Steven Miller once said they must be good because he didn't get many in to work on. He figured the least maintenance, the better the product. So, since then, I've had it in the back of my mind that if I ever needed—''

''Okay, save me the explanations. Sorry I asked. Look, Huckleberry. This is Monday, see. Wednesday. Thursday latest, I'll get one of the guys to bring you one. Don't worry about the cost. We'll take the Chevy and make a deal. I'll take care of you like always. Okay?''

His eyes had narrowed, or narrowed as much as a person with such a broad face's eyes could get. For a moment I was tempted to say, ''Make sure its all legal, now.'' But I didn't. Bondesky knew how to walk the line.

My resolve almost faded again though when he yelled at the closed door and one of the riffraff slithered in. ''Huckleberry,'' Bondesky said in his gravelly voice, ''this is Jimmy. He'll make the switch . . . with the cars . . . when I find one for you. I wanted you to meet so you wouldn't be afraid when he shows up. I'll tell him how to find the house.''

Without prior warning I would have been scared to death, in fact. Jimmy was tall and skeletally thin. He had a bald head, not one of the deceptively sexy ones, but a bony protrusion that was half-covered with a dirty bandage wrapped so close to his head that it looked like he had only one ear. He was so eager to please Bondesky that he just grunted and nodded his acceptance of the assignment. I guess. Maybe he was one of the ones who couldn't talk.

''That's too much trouble, Bondesky. I'll just check back by Thursday morning.'' I didn't want that character near my house.

''No trouble. Jimmy's my best man. He'll take care of you.''

That's what I was afraid of.

''Thank you,'' I said and sidestepped Jimmy to take my leave.

''Huckleberry?''

I almost fell as I tried to turn and avoid touching

Jimmy at the same time. "What?" I asked.

"What color you want?"

Holding my breath so I wouldn't breathe in the same air as Jimmy, I squeaked, "Surprise me," and left.

# Eighteen

I didn't have any other place to go, so I went home and took a bath. I'd had one last night before Stephen called, but after thirty minutes with Bondesky and company, I felt dirty again, deep-down dirty.

Spring storm clouds were gathering once more as I came downstairs to fix a late lunch. I looked outside, but didn't see Joaquin. The sky was turning dark as the clouds swept by like ghost riders, and I turned on the kitchen light before daring to reach inside the pantry for a can of tuna.

The can felt like the right size, but I was disgusted to find it was water chestnuts. "Why would I buy water chestnuts?" I asked myself, my voice sounding strange in the gloom that preceded the coming storm. Summing all my strength, I reached back in the pantry for another can the same size. It was tuna. I wondered how it would taste with water chestnuts.

It was okay; crunchy like apples, but with no real flavor.

What with fixing and eating the sandwich and then cleaning up the small mess I'd made, I was unaware of the size of the approaching turbulence outside. All of a sudden, it was terribly quiet, just like they say about the calm before the storm, and I shivered. But not just from the weather. With the same surety I had felt on Thursday night that I was alone in the house with Steven Miller's body, I now knew that I was not alone.

What to do?

I could cross over the short distance to the back door and run outside into the now-pelting rain, or I could stand right where I was and wait for someone to push open the swinging door from the dining room, or I could . . .

There were footsteps heading my way. I'd never make it to the outside door, and I couldn't just stand there like a helpless victim.

I hid in the pantry.

All the nameless fears of my childhood descended upon me as I shut myself into the tiny area. My heart was beating so furiously at finding myself voluntarily entombed in the most dreaded spot of my house that I couldn't breathe. And with my head swimming from the dizziness of the lack of oxygen and fear, I could barley hear the footsteps of the unknown intruder. I gasped in air, holding my hand over my mouth to cover the sound.

The back door was opened, and I could hear the heavy rainfall. I thought maybe he'd go on out, but then I heard the refrigerator door open, and after a few seconds, close.

He was still in the house.

After some kitchen type noises and the sound of the dining room door swinging to and fro again, I relaxed my position. I had been standing on tiptoe, one hand clutching the miniature doorknob, holding the door shut in case he tried to enter. Stepping back on my heels and taking a deep breath sent me into another spiral of breathless terror; I was still in the pantry, it's narrow width and dead odors sending renewed chills up my spine.

If I moved backward, I'd hit my head on the underside of the staircase. To the sides were the can-loaded shelves. Sweat broke out on my forehead as I fought claustrophobia. Anything was better than this. I started to open the door when I heard another noise. Disoriented now, I didn't know if it came from the kitchen or above me. I was afraid to stay in the pantry but certain I would be killed if I didn't.

After about thirty minutes of crouching in a stiff, defensive position, my legs started to cramp. Nauseous with the stale smells surrounding me, I swayed as I tentatively reached out to actually touch the sides. Supporting myself by holding on to one of the shelves, I shook out first one leg and then, reversing handholds, the other.

I heard the distant thunder—or was it someone on the steps above me?

*I can sit down,* I thought. *Yes, I can.*

No, I couldn't.

Finally, I had to.

Occasionally, when I mopped the kitchen floor, I had opened the pantry and taken a few quick swipes inside. Just enough to push dust and dirt and who knows what else back up under the stairs, I realized as I sat down heavily, bumping my head on a lower upside-down stair. The debris of my mopping efforts and probably of more years than that greeted my hands as I touched the floor to shift to a more comfortable position. I shuddered as I rubbed my hands together, trying to rid them of the gritty trash.

Sitting with my knees crossed, not daring to think what I was sitting on, I held my hands outstretched on my lap like a physician preparing to don surgical gloves for an operation. I was surprised that my back was as comfortable as it was; I had imagined that the pantry extended all the way back in a descending order to the last step, but I seemed to be leaning against some kind of board. I leaned my weight against it and waited.

My thoughts were of whoever was in my house—upstairs or wherever—and to help me forget where I was, I remembered how Stephen and I had finished our phone call last night.

He'd been fascinated by the origin of the poem game; wanted to know immediately where Steven Hyatt was now, disappointed when I told him Australia.

"Did anyone else know about the game?"

"Not that I know. Maybe Steven told. But why would he? It's only a silly game."

"He travels a lot in Europe, you say?"

"Yes, his biggest fans are in Europe. London. Paris."

"Not Italy?"

"I don't know. I don't remember Italy."

Confined in the pantry with my thoughts, I drew my knees up under my chin. Maybe there was something about Steven that I had missed telling Stephen. Again, there was no similarity to their names in my mind.

I leaned against the supporting board, and all thoughts of either man vanished as it cracked and split and I fell backward into an enveloping softness that scared me so much I reached my arms up, searching for a brace, and encountered a spidery string. I jerked my hand away, pulling the string with me. There was a click and the pantry was filled with the light of a small-wattage bulb.

I didn't know there was a light in the pantry.

Now I could see what I had been avoiding for years . . . for a lifetime.

About six cans in from the door, everything seemed to be in some sort of order. After that, the shelves deteriorated into a curious mixture of rusted cans with bug-eaten labels and older glass jars of something once preserved and stored away, but that now supported rusty lids and cloudy contents. A few were cracked, probably from the internal pressure of fermentation; that explained the source of some of the moldy odors.

I was so embarrassed; the floor was nasty, needlessly so. If I had overcome my fear and ever cleaned it just once, the dread and power of the pantry would hopefully have disappeared. Instead, I had let my mother's paranoia overwhelm me and become my own.

In the dregs of the waste on the floor was a mousetrap. If I'd moved my hand a little to the left while I was in the dark, it would have sprung and caught me. I shoved it away with the toe of my shoe, scooting it through the trash by its base. When I moved my shoulder, the board behind me finished its crash to the floor. I held my breath, sure that it had been heard elsewhere in the house.

Nothing. No sound. But I knew he hadn't left.

I twisted around to look at the broken plank. It was really just a plywood slat that had covered the silver-and-pink insulation that was now visible without its protective wood.

That was odd. Why would anyone insulate under the stairs? I thought insulation was for outside walls.

As tentative as I had made my explorations earlier in the dark, I reached forward and poked the shiny side of the wrappings. My finger thrust through the worn and brittle outer layer, making a hole the size a mouse could live in.

Like a mouse, I tore and worried at the edges of the opening until it gave in little pieces, exposing more wadding behind it. Only it wasn't more insulation. It was money. It was what Steven Bondesky would call ''big bucks.''

I'd found my real inheritance.

# Nineteen

In the three hours I was enclosed in the pantry, I weathered my greatest nightmare and my fondest dream: there was a prowler in my house, and I had found a buried treasure.

At first, I pulled out the bills—all hundreds—one at a time, letting them fall in my lap any old way, but when they started to overflow my skirt, I began again, separating the bills in little piles. I was going to arrange them in a thousand a stack, but when that mounted too quickly, I went to ten thousand only to find that amount increased too rapidly, also. I doubled the first piles and came up with my own way to measure the money.

"One Plymouth Voyager, two Plymouth Voyager, three Plymouth Voyager . . ." No wonder Bondesky thought I could buy a Cadillac; I could buy a fleet of Cadillacs.

I knew Bondesky knew about the money, and all this time the fat old man thought I knew about it, too.

"Ten Plymouth Voyager." I stopped.

The phone was ringing.

*The answering machine will catch it,* I thought. And then, *Wonder what time it is?* Stephen was going to call.

Was there was something wrong with the machine, or had I not switched it on? It rang and rang and rang, and I pulled and counted and pulled and counted and pulled and counted.

The ringing stopped.

*He'll call back,* I thought greedily.

Twenty-four Plymouth Voyager. I stopped again.

Someone was coming in the back door. I could hear heavy footsteps crossing the porch. I had forgotten about the intruder.

Hurriedly, I laid half of the split board over the piled-up cash and upended the other half to cover the now enlarged opening where the money seemed to go back under the stairs forever; I hadn't begun to touch it.

Belatedly, I remembered the dim lightbulb and reached for the string to turn it off just as the pantry door opened.

"Honey? Are you all right? What are you doing in there?" It was the first time Joaquin had called me Honey.

I scrambled to my feet, putting a grimy finger to my lips as I warned him, "Shh. There's someone in the house."

Unsteady, I fell against him, and he caught me and drew me out into the kitchen. "Where are they?" he whispered.

Well, now I didn't know. I had been so busy counting money for the last—How long?—that I couldn't remember when I'd heard the last noise from . . . "Upstairs." I pointed.

Together, for I wouldn't obey his instructions to stay put, we sneaked through the downstairs, paused in the front hall, and gingerly climbed the stairs. I was so close that if Joaquin had stopped in midstep, he would have put his foot down on mine.

My room . . . bathroom . . . war room . . . Mother's room . . . even the upstairs sleeping porch. No one.

"Are you sure there was someone here?"

"Yes, but it was hours ago."

"You've been in that pantry all this time?" He couldn't believe it.

"Oh, it wasn't so bad," I said.

"No? You'd better take a look at yourself," and he pointed to the bathroom.

Well, I did have to go.

I closed the bathroom door and then opened it a crack. "You'll stay right here, won't you? You won't leave me up here alone?"

He moved from the hall into my bedroom. "I'll be right here," he said reassuringly. We were speaking in normal tones now.

"Good golly, Miss Molly," I looked like one of the mice who'd died in Father's traps. Cobwebs in my hair were the least of the smutty and foul rubbish I found covering my head and sundress.

"Ugh . . . yuck . . . ooh . . . ow," was all I could utter as I shed my dress and filled the sink. I kicked the discarded garment with my toe: another sundress down the drain. A lot of black and gray goopy things peeled off my hands and arms and—yuck again—my face. I thought I was going to vomit, and I brushed my hair so hard, it stood on end like Little Orphan Annie's.

Only the realization that Joaquin was waiting kept me

from completely stripping and bathing. How many baths could a person take a day? I took a cotton housecoat off the hook on the bathroom door and wrapped it around me.

Joaquin laughed when I entered the bedroom. "I can't tell if you look worse now or before."

"I think there are dead things in that pantry," I said laughing with him. *And money—lots of money,* my heart sang.

"Would you like me to clean it out for you?"

"Oh, no. No . . . no. I'm responsible for the condition it's in; I'll clean it up. Obviously, its a long overdue chore. Joaquin?" I hesitated, then went on. "Why were you in the house? Were you looking for me?"

He straightened up and almost seemed hurt I had asked. "After the rain stopped, I was checking the garden. I kept hearing your phone ring and knowing you were home—"

"How did you know I was home?"

"I saw your car through the clinic's garage window. Anyway, the back door was open, and I was worried about you. I was going to search the house, but then I heard something in the pantry . . ." He paused and looked at me strangely. "Honey, the phone did ring forever. Didn't you hear it?" And then quickly. "Have I done something wrong?"

"No. I didn't know the rain stopped. Yes, I heard the phone ringing, and I don't know why, either. I mean, why it would keep on ringing like that, unless I didn't remember to switch on the machine?" I walked over to the night table. "No, it's on. What do you think could . . . Oh, my God."

"What's wrong?"

"There's no answering tape."

"It's run out?"

"No, I mean it's gone. Look." We both looked at the empty sprockets inside the guts of the machine.

"Maybe you took it out."

"Don't be stupid," I said sharply and then just as quickly added, "I'm sorry, Joaquin. I don't know what's wrong with me. I'm not as nice as I used to be. I meant to say, no, I would never do that, and if I had for any reason, I would have remembered it. No. Whoever was in the house took it. But why?"

"What was on it?" he asked moving toward the front window.

I sat down on the edge of the bed, rubbing my forehead, trying to remember. "The last time it was on was . . . when . . . when Ste . . . a friend called last night, and it clicked on before I could catch it."

"Would it have recorded your conversation?"

"Yes, at least thirty minutes of it. I've done it before, and all you have to do is hit Erase. It resets itself, but why would . . . oh, my God."

"What? You scare me when you say that."

"Nothing," I answered. I could only guess who would want a taped conversation between Stephen and me, and I didn't like who I was guessing. The somebody we had decided last night who had either followed him from Italy or who already knew the address of the phone number on the piece of paper. My number.

Joaquin acted hurt again because I was hiding something from him, and he knew it. "Well, I guess you're okay now. I'll go. Unless you want to report the missing tape to the police . . . to Silas Sampson?"

"Joaquin, I'm sorry," I said again. "I don't mean to

act so secretive, but there's a lot going on around here that you, a stranger, needn't get involved in. I know you want to help, but that's one of the reasons I don't want you to move in upstairs. The last person who said they'd be responsible for me . . . for the house . . . was Steven Miller, and he's dead because of it. And I don't want that . . . or anything else bad to happen to another living soul, not to you or anyone, because of me." I looked up from where I had been staring at the threadbare rag rug on my bedroom floor and said, "Joaquin. Joaquin, did you hear me?"

He was still standing in front of the window, his back to me and his head cocked to one side. With one hand, he waved at me, signaling me to be quiet. "Listen," he whispered.

I listened and heard a noise like someone dragging a heavy piece of furniture across the floor.

We looked up. It was coming from the third floor.

"You stay here," he said and ran from the room.

We reached the downstairs landing about the same time. After all, it's my house, and I knew just how to take the steps three at a time, even if I hadn't tried it until after my mother and father died.

Joaquin glared at me but didn't take the time to stop me again. We ran outside and up the wooden steps. He grabbed me by my coattail and pushed me behind him. Quietly, he tried the door. It was unlocked. Joaquin turned the knob slowly, then charged through the door like Silas Sampson.

"What the devil?" a voice exclaimed.

"Who are you?" asked Joaquin.

I peeked under his upraised arm, gave a squeal, and ran under it, feeling the brush of his fingertips as he tried to grab me. I heard him gasp as I jumped in the middle of the beanbag chair the stranger was sitting in and gave him a big kiss.

"Lydia, my own sweet girl. I'm home. You're a sight for sore eyes." The object of my affection hugged me tight and looked up at Joaquin. "In answer to your question, mate. I'm Steven Hyatt. Who are you?"

# Twenty

"Steven. Steven . . . Steven . . . Steven." All I could do was hug my friend around his neck and babble his name. Touching him was like reaching out and grabbing a piece of something that had been missing from my life not just this last crazy week, but for a long time.

When I could finally halt the mindless dribble of Stevens gushing from my mouth, I began to ask questions that had their origins in the same never-never land of simplicity and borderline lunacy saying, "How did you get in? How long have you been here? How long can you stay?" Yes, and I even heard myself say, "Where did you come from?"

But Steven didn't let me down. He answered them all just as if they merited the same dignity as legitimate, intelligent questions. "With my key. All day. Until I have to go." And, surprisingly, "New York."

"Oh," I said. "I thought Australia."

"Australia?" He frowned, his forehead crinkling from the effort to look serious, but nothing could ever make

Steven Hyatt look serious or older. He had shut his eyes to exaggerate the thoughtfulness he had given his supposed place of residence, and when he opened them, I saw the same sparkle in his green eyes that I had seen and appreciated seventeen years earlier. His hair, a ball of brown, curly fuzz that matched mine in unruliness, if not in color, seemed a little longer than it had back in the freshman speech class where we had met, and the glasses that gripped his long, thin face were now wire-rimmed aviators.

I didn't know way back then that Steven's colorless, plastic frames and off-the-chart IQ scores contributed to his title of Nerd of all Nerdos. From my sheltered point of view, I not only did not know Steven was a nerd, I didn't know there was such a thing. Nobody ever bothered to tell me.

The harmonious glance and smile we shared in Miss Mott's class and an identical one later after school were probably the first friendly eye contacts either Steven or I had ever exchanged with anyone in our first two weeks at Paschal High School. I smiled again when I recognized him in his green Pontiac trying to maneuver out of the congested parking lot, and he grinned back just as I ducked into the passenger side of my father's car.

As usual, Father was so afraid of being late that he had been early, waiting forty-five minutes for me in the hot sun. I had told him repeatedly that I wasn't going anywhere after school and I would be right there waiting for him, no matter what time he showed up, but he continued to come early because I might get hot waiting for him. I was fifteen and healthy. He was old and had only three more years to live.

"Your friend is following us," my father said.

"What?" I stared at Father.

"Your friend, the one you smiled with when you got in the car," my father said as he looked up at the rear-view mirror.

I first tried to look through the same mirror, but the reverse image confused me, so I finally scrunched up enough nerve to turn my head around. Steven saw me and waved casually—too casual to really be casual—that kind of wave. We were on Rosedale, almost home; he was following us.

"He's not my friend," I protested. "I just saw him today for the first time in speech class."

Father turned into the driveway. "What an impression my little girl makes on boys. One smile and they follow her all the way home."

I jumped out of the car, determined to make a run for the house, but Father stopped me. "Honey, you have a visitor." Steven had parked and was getting out of his car, coming toward us.

"Hello," I said reluctantly to the approaching boy.

"Hello," said Steven. "I'm Steven Hyatt." He held out his hand to Father. He didn't look at me.

"I'm Joseph Huckleberry. This is my daughter, Honey. I understand you have a speech class together at R. L. Paschal High School?"

"Yes, sir. I followed you home to tell you that I wasn't following you home. That is, I was behind you, not following you, when I noticed that we were getting closer to home . . . farther away from school. Well, I know it looked like I was following you, so I thought I had better follow you to tell you I wasn't. Following you, that is." Steven stopped to take a breath.

"And where do you live, Steven Hyatt?" asked my father.

Steven pointed his long, bony arm toward Rosedale. "Back there . . . two blocks back on South Adams."

"I see," said my father, and it was only years after his death that I realized that he did see and understand, but at the time, I thought he was being his usual polite self when he said, "I see." Then, "Honey, I'm going to take Steven Hyatt upstairs to my office and show him our toys. You go on in and say hello to your mother; then bring us up some lemonade. That sound all right to you, Steven Hyatt?"

Father never called him anything but the full Steven Hyatt as in, "Honey, Steven Hyatt is going to take you to school and bring you home every day. We have negotiated a small fee for this service with which we both are agreeable." Or, "Honey, it is all right for Steven Hyatt to study with you on the third floor while I read my paper there."

Steven Hyatt lived with an elderly aunt who had taken him in because of need, not love. She wasn't mean or cruel, she just forgot he was there, and he was incredibly lonely. We read books together, acted out plays, and started our unknown poet game in the spacious, chopped-up third floor of my strange house.

I remember the day we worked out the intricacies of the game. We were laughing at the poem "The Optimist." I recited:

*The optimist fell ten stories*
*At each window bar*
*He shouted to his friends:*

Before I could finish, Steven jumped up and shouted, " 'All right so far!' "

We laughed harder than the humor warranted, but I've noticed since that the young and the innocent tend to do that; that being funny is more fun than what's funny.

"Okay, smarty," I had told Steven. "See if you can get this one. 'How far is it called to the grave?' "

"Get what?" asked Steven.

"The next line. Since you're so clever, tell me the next line after 'How far is it called to the grave?' "

"Oh," he said, "do you mean, 'The child looked up from its play'? Or, 'The lover looked up with a smile'? Or perhaps, Miss Honey, you were referring to 'The mother looked up with a tear'. Was that the one?"

"You missed one," I said.

"Oh, no, I didn't." Steven rose up again from one of the overstuffed beanbag chairs my father had bought us and knelt before me, head bowed and dramatically recited, " 'It is only a life, dear friend.' "

"Yes, that's it. You've got it, Steven."

After that, all our phone calls began with the first line of a poem, the Unknowns being our particular favorites because we could use our imaginations to fashion a life for them.

To other teenagers, it would have seemed a strange relationship, but given the way I was reared and how starved Steven was for company, it seemed ours was the normal way. No popular television shows, no loud music, no secret drinking and pot smoking ever seeped into our lives. We just weren't cool. Except to each other.

I thought Steven knew everything, and our conversations might be about politics or the environment or a nuance in a poem. No subject was too sacred. I knew no matter what I said, Steven would never laugh at me, never make fun of my views or my not knowing something.

"Steven, are you a virgin?"

"Yes, Honey, I am."

"Am I?"

"Yes, you are. But why do you have to ask?"

"This book says Elizabeth was called the Virgin Queen, but it was alleged that she had several lovers. I was wondering if maybe I misunderstood what a virgin was after all, and maybe I really wasn't one."

So he told me in very clinical terms what a virgin was.

"I thought so. I thought that's what it was all about. Steven, do you think we'll ever do that?"

"You mean together?"

"Yes. No. I mean just do it with somebody?"

"I hope so, Honey." Steven grinned. " 'Cause that will mean we're normal, healthy people, and sometimes I wonder about us, so that would be reassuring. But with each other? Nah, I don't think so."

"Why not, Steven?"

"Because I think we love each other too much, Honey."

I've always done my best thinking in bed, so before I went to sleep that night, I thought about what Steven had said, and somewhere in my mind, I thought I understood what he meant. We were too close to ever be lovers, but we would always be the best of friends. But what really made me blush was when I remembered that my father had sat in his recliner, not ten feet away from us, ostensibly reading the newspaper he held in front of his face.

Had my father heard us talking about sex? Did it matter? Did he ever pay attention to anything we said?

# Twenty-one

Sometimes I wonder if relationships like mine with Steven Hyatt still exist—an extended period of innocence incongruent with the rest of the world; our pretended realities were our truth, and the real truths were tolerated by us only until we could return to the ones of our own making.

Sometimes I'm not sure Steven and I ever made it all the way back. He writes and directs his plays and movies with an inward eye that is hailed as creative by the critics, but I recognize its warped origin, and I balance carefully between productive and dysfunctional lifestyles.

Had our three years on the third floor marked us? Or would we have been the same without them?

That the past week had strained me beyond my capabilities was a surprise to me, but I knew it when I saw Steven. My first thoughts were to curl up in his arms and cry, like a child does when its mother shows up after a crisis.

But Steven was being a good host to Joaquin. He

acted as if the dusty, hodgepodge rooms were his, and Joaquin was an invited guest popping in for brandy. No, it was beer Steven was offering.

Joaquin accepted.

I tried to tune in to their conversation when I caught Steven staring at me in a concerned way.

"Murdered! No!" he said.

Oh, Joaquin was telling him about Steven Miller. I couldn't remember if Steven Hyatt knew Steven Miller or not.

"Honey," Steven turned as if to comfort me for Steven Miller's murder as if it just had occurred this minute, not five days ago.

I waved him away. "You're not getting away with it, Steven Hyatt."

"What?" he exclaimed innocently.

"Australia. You were in Australia. I may not remember what day it is without my Day-Timer, but I do distinctly remember you telling me that you were going on location in Australia for that new script of yours . . . the . . . the . . . something or other about you-know-what."

He laughed, "You mean *The Playful Platypus Ponders Paradise in Perth*? That one?"

I ignored him. "You were there," I said, remembering. "I called your hotel. They said you were on safari somewhere out in the outback, a reserve or reservoir, or something like that. What are you doing here, Steven?"

Steven leaned forward and said, "Not now, Honey. Not in front of the g-u-e-s-t." Still leaning toward me, he cut his eyes around at Joaquin and said, "Who is he, anyway?"

If I had been Joaquin, I would have left after introductions were made, but the gardener lingered as if he still didn't trust me with Steven, who offered him another beer from the Styrofoam cooler at the end of the couch.

Steven loved to talk and show off, and since this was the first time we'd ever had a stranger on the third floor, he gave Joaquin a guided tour like it was the House of Wax. "You notice there are no doors up here? The original plan called for doors, but since Mr. Huckleberry never finished it out, he never installed them."

He paused at the opening to the largest of the side rooms. "This was Mr. Huckleberry's workroom."

"What great models," Joaquin exclaimed as he gazed at the collection of meticulously constructed pieces of wood and metal.

"Yeah." I caught a note of familial pride in Steven's voice. "Honey always thought these were toys Mr. H. made just for her to play with, but I've always thought they were the best in the business."

*What business?* I thought. "They are toys," I declared and then added with purpose, "my toys."

"Look at this," Joaquin had switched on one of the gadgets, one with fine wires and pulleys, and despite its disuse for over a decade, we watched it smoothly hoist and then lower a small platform with only a small whine to indicate its activity.

"That's my doll elevator," I said.

The men looked silently at me, then at each other.

"What about this one," Steven said, pointing out a round, dust-covered object.

Joaquin whistled. "It ought to be in a museum."

"That's my spinning wheel," I said, realizing that my voice sounded like a petulant three-year-old.

"No, Honey, this is a prototype of a mechanized system that revolutionized its industry." Steven grinned at Joaquin. "No telling how far back these things go. Look in this cabinet. And down here."

I had heard Steven explain to me before that my father was a patent engineer and researcher, that the models weren't actually toys as my father had told me. He had continued to build them way past the time that I was interested in such play. But as I looked at the cobweb-encrusted geegaws and thingamabobs, I remembered the hours Father had spent, bent over the miniature pieces of wood or metal, carving, bending, and fitting the intricate parts together. He'd built them for me, he'd told me.

"All his blueprints are in here," Steven told Joaquin as he opened one large cabinet pigeonholed with dozens of tightly rolled pieces of brittle paper.

Joaquin shook his head in disbelief as he stared at the array and then suddenly, he said, "My God." And he stooped to inspect one of the models on a lower shelf. He was talking to Steven about it when I noticed something strange about the shape of the back pocket of his blue jeans. I knew he smoked, but I didn't think I had ever seen Joaquin chewing tobacco. Because of his half-crouched position, the shape of what appeared to be a tin showed through the pocket stretched tight against his hip.

My thoughts echoed Joaquin's. *My God.* That was no can of nasty chewing tobacco in his pocket. It was only its location that had caused me to think of a tobacco tin. The slight bulge in his back pocket was smaller. Rectangular. It looked like a tape cassette, a miniature tape cassette, like the one that had disappeared only a half hour ago from my answering machine downstairs. It was so clearly impressed against the fabric of Joaquin's worn jeans that I could even see the indention of the tiny reels.

I knew I wasn't mistaken. Joaquin had taken my tape. But why?

"Do you mind if I look for the blueprint that matches this one?" Joaquin asked Steven. "It reminds me of something."

"No, I don't mind." He turned to me. "Honey, is it okay with you? Honey?" Then more concerned. "Lydia?"

I had walked back into the main room, trying to figure out why Joaquin would have taken the tape while I was in the bathroom and then lied about it. My heart hurt. Instinctively, I had trusted the gardener Ralph had found for our combined lawns, had felt safe inside with him working outside and, for goodness sakes, had even invited him to share a meal with me—something I had never done before in my life. I had never even let Steven Hyatt eat a tuna sandwich on my back porch, much less in my kitchen, and here I had gone and fixed linguini with clam sauce for a stranger who stole from me five minutes after he'd come up my stairs.

Why would he steal that tape?

Then my heart froze and I caught a ragged breath. My conversation with Stephen X was on that tape.

"Honey?"

Steven had followed me. As I sank down on one of the couches, he knelt beside me, taking my hands in his. "What's the matter?"

We could hear Joaquin rustling papers in the other room.

I wasn't ready, not with Joaquin so close, to tell

Steven about what was really bothering me, so instead I replied, "Were you downstairs earlier?"

"Yeah, I came in to get some ice from the fridge. Why? Were you at home? I thought you were gone, so I didn't bother to ring the doorbell. I just used the key you gave me. Were you home? Did I scare you? I'm sorry, Honey. Why didn't you call out?"

"Tell me about Australia," I said.

He reached over to smooth down the red curls that still spiraled from my head after the vigorous brushing I had given them to remove real or imagined bugs and other assorted pantry gunk. I could tell he was thinking about what he was going to tell me, then his eyes rolled resignedly and he answered, "I didn't want to bother you, but—"

"You're in trouble."

Steven laughed and sank down beside me on the couch. "How did you know?"

"How could I not?" I patted his hand. "Money?" I questioned.

Steven Hyatt was a genius. He could write, direct, and produce some of the most avant-garde films of the century, but he spent money as fast as he generated it on the next project that caught his fancy. To his credit, they were all lucrative, but the lucre just didn't stay with him long.

"I borrowed money from the wrong people," he confessed to me as he burrowed deeper into the safe confines of the worn, comfortable couch. "Then, when I made it back, I put it into this Australian venture before I gave them a chance to look at it."

"The script?"

"No, their money."

I didn't have to ask who "they" were or if they were mad at Steven, or how mad they were. Heck, I read a lot and watch some television. I know you don't cross the "thems" of the world, but I relaxed some. Steven had been in this kind of mess before, so I only half-listened as he finished up.

"And so they think I'm still in Australia with my crew." He suddenly sat up straight. "Hey, you don't think they'll do anything to my crew, do you?" Then he noticed my inattention to his problems.

"I'm sorry, Honey. I've been going on and on about the usual, and here you're involved in a murder and running up and down stairs like an aging Nancy Drew with a dark, foreign-looking man who knows an awful lot about engineering to only be the gardener. Tell me, Lydia, dear," he whispered it in a joking manner, not realizing how close his words were to my own thoughts. "Did the gardener do it?"

But, "An aging Nancy Drew?" was all I shouted at him. I playfully smothered him with a sofa pillow, which, judging from the amount of dust motes it released, was guaranteed to give him a fatal asthma attack if I couldn't manage to snuff out his breath with it first.

"Pardon me."

We quit our wrestling to look around for the source of the voice. Ah, how could we have forgotten about Joaquin, he of the dubious garden-plot plot and recent tape burglary?

He was leaning against the door frame, his big body curved in a relaxed pose, like a ballerina's at the bar. "I've been rude," he said. "You guys haven't seen each other for a long time. You don't need to be entertaining me. Don't bother, Miss Huckleberry, I'll let myself out.'' He reached his hand out to Steven. ''I'm glad our burglar turned out to be friendly.'' He walked out the door, nodding his dark head in an affable fashion. If he'd had a hat, he would have tipped it.

''Mexican?'' asked Steven. '' 'You guys!' Gimme a break.''

''From California,'' I said.

''Oh, well then,'' he said.

# Twenty-two

The doorbell rang at 7:30 Tuesday morning, too early for man, beast, or me, since Steven Hyatt and I had stayed up until nearly three talking and catching up on things. But not too early for Janie Bridges. Her straw-colored pageboy swung loosely in the morning breeze as she vigorously attacked the key-shaped knob of the old-fashioned doorbell.

''Janie!'' I tried not to sound as surprised as I felt at seeing her on my front porch. ''What are you doing here?'' I asked, hoping it didn't sound too rude to ask.

''Why, I've come for the funeral,'' she answered as instant frown lines appeared between her blue eyes. ''Aren't you going? Of course, you're going. You are going to Steven Miller's funeral, aren't you?''

My hand went to my throat. ''Is it today? But Silas said he would call me . . . Never mind,'' I said, suddenly remembering the status of my answering machine. ''Come in. Come in. What time is the funeral, and how did you know about it?''

Janie came inside, and as I followed her into the living room, I said, "I didn't know you were going to Steven Miller's funeral."

"Oh, yes, I wouldn't miss it," Janie replied as if going to strange men's funeral services were the most natural thing in the world. "I want to see the murderer."

"Pardon?"

"The murderer. They always show up at the funeral. Can't keep them away. Trust me, they're always there." She sat her plump self down on the pink couch, holding her black patent purse in front of her.

They, they, they. I knew too many "theys" and "thems." There was Peggy at the cleaner's "they," which translated into cops ("they" were the ones who had sent the handsome Silas). And Steven Hyatt's mention of "them" was decidedly the underworld or loan-sharking mobsters who controlled everything the legal "theys" didn't. Now here was Janie's "they," this time a murderer.

"Do you really think they'll be there?" I asked as I offered to take Janie's purse. She shook her head, indicating she'd hold on to the suitcase-sized article, and as she chattered knowledgeably about the nefarious habits of malefactors, I looked around for a place to sit. The effort reminded me once again of how unaccustomed I had been such a short while ago to having guests in the house. Finally, clutching my terry robe close with my hands—I don't know what happened to the sash—I chose one of the green velvet Queen Anne chairs.

"You can take these, though," said Janie, and she handed me a large sack of what I recognized as West's pride and joy: a bag full of kolaches.

"Great," I said. "I'll make some coffee, and I'll ask

Steven if he wants some. I've told him about Czech cooking, but—''

''Steven!'' screamed Janie.

''What?'' I shouted, startled by her scream.

''You said Steven. Have you met him? Is he here?'' She turned and twisted on the couch, trying to peer through the murky light of the living room for a body she might have missed.

''Oh, you mean Stephen.''

''Yes. Your Italian Steven. The one I've been researching.''

''No, Janie. This is my Texas Steven I'm talking about.'' And I carefully spelled the difference to her, which, I was gratified to note, she understood perfectly.

''Then let's call him—the one upstairs—Steven Hyatt, so we won't get confused. Honey, do you mind if I make it lighter in here?'' she asked, and in answer I twisted the switch on the red lamp; she jumped up and raised the shades, the resulting sunlight making both of us blink and squint for a minute.

''There, that's better,'' Janie said even though it wasn't. When we could finally see again, she looked around the room in ernest and exclaimed, ''Honey, my God, this room.''

I sighed and decided to ignore her outburst. I wasn't up to explaining my living room.

''So, how did you find out about Steven Miller's funeral?'' I asked.

Still rubbernecking, this time around the wide doorway into the dining room, Janie answered, ''The *Star-Telegram* obits. You know I read them every day. There was a small notice about Miller's services today at ten. I just decided I'd come on up to Fort Worth and go with you. It's not often I get real hands-on with a case, you know."

"What about your bookstore? Did you close Pages?"

"I put a Gone Sleuthing sign on the door." Her eyes finally came back to mine. "Besides, I wanted to tell you all what I've found out about S-t-e-p-h-e-n X in person."

"Okay, but first I want some coffee." I told her I'd be right back, and still in my short cotton gown and wide-open robe, I went outside and up the stairs to beat on the third-floor door. Steven Hyatt didn't open it immediately, but ultimately my persistence penetrated his sleep, and he stood in the doorway in a white T-shirt and colorful, plaid boxer shorts.

"You're going to have to come down and entertain my friend Janie while I get dressed for a funeral," I told him. "I'll make some coffee. She brought breakfast, so come on down. Now."

"Okay, okay," he groaned through half-opened eyes, and he started down the stairs behind me.

I was nearly at the bottom—right past the second floor—when I realized he was behind me. I turned and held up a restraining hand, which caught the still mostly asleep man in the chest as he continued to half-fall down the steps. "No, stupid. Go get dressed, then come down."

This was when Silas walked around the side of the house.

"Honey?" Silas's voice was tentative. "Are you all right?"

"Silas," I said. Brightly.

"Silas?" Steven said. Not so brightly, but I certainly

thought friendly enough. He opened both his eyes and held out his hand. ''Steven Hyatt.''

''Steven Hyatt?'' asked Silas, coming up the few remaining steps to shake Steven's hand, but turning to look at me. ''Steven Hyatt of the 'Let's all come to the grave, my friend' telephone calls?''

'' 'How far is it called to the grave?' '' I corrected.

'' 'It's only a life, dear friend,' '' Steven replied, and for one long beat, we smiled and stared into one another's eyes, remembering.

''Welcome home from Australia, Mr. Hyatt,'' said Silas.

''Thank you, it's good to be here,'' answered my friend.

''Think you can answer a few questions . . . just routine, of course?'' Silas asked Steven.

Steven looked at me.

''Its okay,'' I said. ''He's a detective. Silas Sampson.''

Steven still looked blank.

Impatient, I snapped, ''Its about Steven Miller. You know. The murder.''

''Oh, sure, sure, come on up. Honey, you said something about coffee?'' Silas and I watched as Steven's thin but muscular legs strutted back up the steps.

''I can explain, Silas.''

''Later.'' He looked at me again, his eyes taking in the rumpled look of me. I certainly wasn't looking my best around men these days. ''Are you going to bring up some coffee?'' he asked as he followed Steven.

''No.''

''No?'' He turned and stared down at me.

''No,'' I said again, ''but you and Steven are welcome

to come down and have a cup with me and my friend, Janie. Which by the way, Mr. Detective Silas Sampson, is what I had come outside to tell my friend, Steven Hyatt, just before you arrived.'' I started toward the front door. ''By the way again,'' I shouted up at him, ''it's not eight o'clock yet. What are you doing here?''

''I came to tell you about Steven Miller's funeral this morning. At ten o'clock. I tried to call you last night, but your answering machine is broken.''

''I knew that,'' I said, and I left with him wondering if I meant I knew about Steven Miller's funeral or about the malfunctioning machine.

Janie was trying to fix the coffee using the old metal percolator left over from the aunts' time in the house. ''It's like camping out,'' she told me as she assembled the various parts of the pot.

I sneaked a peek as I reached inside the pantry for coffee. The loose boards still covered the you-know-what, but with new strangers in the house—making themselves at home no less—I'd have to take care of the little windfall I'd discovered the day before. ''It makes good coffee,'' I assured Janie as she filled the pot with water. ''Think of it as a permanent Mr. Coffee filter.''

''Don't get smart with me,'' she laughed. ''I was fixing coffee in this kind of pot before you were born, but I gotta admit it's been a while. There.'' She put the pot on the gas burner. ''Hope I remember how to know when it's done.'' Looking at me, she snorted, ''Why, I swear, Honey, you're not dressed yet. Run on, now. I'll set these out.'' And she grabbed at the baker's sack as I skedaddled upstairs.

''Nothing fancy,'' I heard her call up the stairwell to

my room. "Just your basic black will do. Like mine."

What to do.

There was nothing black in my closet, and I didn't know where in the world to look in the war room for something suitable to wear to a funeral. It just goes to show you. You think you're so organized—I looked at the neat, shrouded rows of clothes hanging there—and then something unexpected happens like a man dying in your living room, and the next thing you know, you need black clothes to wear to a funeral.

I finally found a full, black cotton skirt in a bag marked Fall—Second Week, which made me look too young, and a black cotton sweater in a four-weeks-later bag, which might make me too hot. The costume did nothing for my slight curves, but hey, what did that matter? It was more important to dress the part.

Silas, Steven Hyatt, and Janie were sitting around my dining room table eating kolaches and drinking what smelled like very strong coffee when I came downstairs. Stopping for a minute at the small door that led in from the hall, I took a long look at the group. *Who are these people,* I thought, *and what are they doing in my house eating and talking like it was the normal thing to do?* Which it wasn't. It was Tuesday, and I should be . . . Where? Oh, no, where should I be?

I was getting ready to bolt back upstairs to check my itinerary when Silas spotted me.

"Honey, we've saved you a sausage whatchamacallit. Janie says they're your favorite."

Janie didn't know, Silas knew but probably didn't remember, but Steven Hyatt knew and remembered. He shrugged his lean shoulders and gave me an apologetic glance. "Maybe it's time," he mouthed using the same phrase he'd uttered last night when I'd complained about the people invasion I'd experienced.

It had been Steven Hyatt, of course, who had taken over when Mother and Father died like they did. He had called Bondesky, who had called the lawyer, who had told me things I didn't understand. I cried, and Bondesky had said, "Christ, who's gonna take care of her?"

And Steven Hyatt had said, "I will."

But I'd been shy about letting him into the house, and we had continued to meet upstairs, and that's where he had written down everything that I was supposed to do for the next week. And then, the next month, and then, the one after that. After that, of course, he was gone, but his schedules kept coming from Austin, some scribbled on the backs of essays he'd written for his university classes, marked A over F. A for content, F for spelling.

And somewhere in the next few years, I'd started writing my own schedules and making my own decisions like what classes to take at TCJC, how to shop for groceries or clothes, and where to get a job. And when to take a lover.

Steven nearly choked when I told him about it during one spring break. "It was absolutely glorious," I said, "but then I realized I really didn't like him, just his body. I used him, Steven."

That was before I had my hair cut and permed, so it just fell over my eyes in a long sweep that Steven Hyatt pushed aside to kiss my forehead and whisper, "No, I don't think so, Honey. I think he got as good as he gave. And you don't see him anymore?"

"No, I felt too guilty. And then, too, he wanted more."

"More? Than what?"

''Steven,'' I said looking seriously into his green eyes, ''he wanted to come into the house.''

I took a deep breath and entered the dining room. Steven Hyatt had the grace to stand and pull out a chair for me. Our eyes met. We both knew I had just passed over a line—a thin line, but a point of demarcation none-theless. From now on, I could never again say that no one ever came into my house.

Silas and Janie were getting on like a house afire. You think you know someone—I'd known Janie four years—and yet, you never really know anyone. Knowing she was a mystery fanatic and seeing her in action were two different things. Her blue eyes squinted, widened, and narrowed again as she listened to Silas go on about his work and himself. He was so wound up, flattered that she was so interested, that words fairly bubbled out of his mouth like oil out of the ground.

I heard a few words I recognized like ''ammo'' and ''bust,'' but Janie kept on nodding when he said things like ''a one eighty-seven'' or ''twist'' or even ''a barrel of little red apples.'' She was in her element, and when Silas went to the kitchen to get more coffee, she leaned over her untouched cup and said, ''I'm in love.'' But in an afterthought, she added in the universal Pegg-at-the-cleaner's code, ''But, Honey, he'll never believe you. He's a good cop, but he won't be able to help you.''

''I know,'' I said, trying to sound like a pro. ''That's what they tell me on the streets.''

# Twenty-three

Janie wore black gloves with her outfit, heavy black ones that reached well past the wrist bone, but not as far as the elbow. She was a little upset that I hadn't any but was mollified a little when I agreed to let her slap a black straw hat, complete with a short, tasteful veil, on my head, where it nestled among my corkscrew curls. She kept the hat in her car trunk for just such emergencies. "You just never know, Honey."

You also never know about funerals.

What I had intended as an unobtrusive, discreet entrance turned into a parade of sorts. Janie led me by my elbow to the front of the funeral parlor—the Millers weren't churchgoers—to greet the family who were doing their duty in a dark, uneven lineup. Steven Hyatt, whom I had insisted accompany us, followed in a black-and-white striped, summer sport coat circa the 1920s. "It's not a costume," he'd insisted. "I wear it every day, and 'sides, it's the only thing I own that's got black in it, unless you let me wear my T-shirt."

Going ahead of me, Janie stage-whispered to the first mourner in line, "I'm Janie Bridges, a friend of Honey Huckleberry's. Here to support her. You know. She found the body." She moved on to the next in line, repeating her litany.

I reached out and took the hand of the man in front of me. Embarrassed by Janie's introduction, I whispered in a real whisper, "I'm sorry about your father."

"Steven Miller," said the young man.

"Yes, I'm sorry about your father . . . Steven Miller."

"No, I'm Steven Miller," he said.

"You're Steven Miller?" I asked incredulously in a normal but very loud sounding voice.

"Yes, I was Steven Miller, Jr., but now I'm just Steven Miller."

"Of course you are," I replied and moved on to the next one, also a man.

"I'm sorry about your . . . your . . . death," I mumbled and ran past the others, pumping hands as I went, Steven Hyatt only nodded as he sidestepped past the group. I caught up with Janie about five relatives down the line.

"Found the body, did you?" a large woman asked as I paused in front of her, hand outstretched.

"Yes." Why deny it now?

I wanted to sink into the nearest pew, but Janie dragged me back toward the end of the rows of the small chapel. "This way we can see everybody," she said. "We can't miss him."

It was downright embarrassing, causing more attention than the corpse, but subsequent mourners were dutifully informed that I—"the one who found him"—was present and identified by "she's the one with the red hair and black hat'' or ''black sweater and red face.'' With red and black being the prime locators.

I genuinely mourned Steven Miller. He had been my friend and protector. He'd died in my house as I had held his hand. I had shared in his death, and I was diminished because of it, but it was obvious that I wasn't going to be allowed to grieve for my friend at his funeral service.

It wasn't real, anyway. Not the flowers I'd sent, the telephone calls I'd made to his widow, or the card I had written legitimized Steven Miller's death. That would only come for me when I saddled up and headed out of Fort Worth on another sales trip at five o'clock in the morning, hitting me when I would stop for gas and a final checkup before moving out. I used to like knowing that Steven Miller and I were the only ones awake in the city. Now I would miss that comfort and miss his customary benediction before my journeys. I would miss him in my life.

We stood to pray, and Janie whipped out a small notepad. I stared at it, wanting to knock it out of her hand. Aghast at her nerve but fascinated by her first entry—achieved only after she'd flipped several pages filled with what looked to be a recipe for either gold or chocolate meringue pie—''IV posbs,'' was scribbled at the top of the blue-lined page balanced in the palm of her hand. When the minister gave everyone permission to sit down, Janie continued to scratch an account of Steven Miller's funeral into her private record.

''HH nervs,'' was the next description of the event.

''You've got that right,'' I whispered into her ear, ''nervous that you're going to get us thrown out of here.'' Then, curious, I pointed to the first inscription.

"What does 'IV' mean? Isn't that a medical term?"

"Four. I think I see four possible suspects."

"You do?" I looked around. "Who are they?"

Janie shook her head. "No. First you tell me who you see."

With everyone now praying from a sitting position, I risked looking around the small but appropriately furnished chapel to see what I could see. I put my hand on my knee, spreading a finger for each "posbs" I counted.

Janie nudged me. "No, Honey, whisper them to me and I'll write them down."

With my mouth in her ear, I related, "Going by your original criteria, which was to see how many people I recognize, here's the list. One. Silas Sampson. He's standing in back, doing the same thing we're doing.

"Then two, me." Janie wrote HH right under Si-Samp. "Oh, and there's Ralph." She looked up and I added, "That's Dr. Ralph Ketchum . . . with a K." I pointed to the top of Ralph's round, neatly combed head, bent in prayer, two pews behind us. "He's the head of the clinic next door, and Steven Miller worked for them, too. I guess he's representing the staff and other doctors."

Suddenly I gasped.

"What? Where?" Janie's head was bobbing from side to side like a doll on a dashboard.

"There on the right. One . . . two . . . three rows down? The guy who looks like he belongs in the funnies? That's Steven Bondesky. I didn't know he knew Steven Miller. No, wait; that's not true. Bondesky pays my bills, and I knew he knew of Steven Miller, but good lord, would you look at that?"

"What? What?"

"There by the door, standing behind Silas. The man with one ear? Or rather, the man with the filthy bandages over one ear? That's Jimmy, the something or other who works for Bondesky."

"Does he smell as bad as he looks?" There's nothing slow about Janie.

"Yes, he does. Wonder what he's doing here?"

Steven Hyatt punched me in the ribs. "Would you two be quiet? You're embarrassing me."

I shut up, but Janie gave him a scathing look and deliberately added, "StvHyt" to her growing list.

With the first note of the postlude, Janie hauled me up and over the last pews so that we were posted by the door when the mourners exited. Steven Hyatt walked right past us, like he didn't know us, and Silas, standing across the floor space from us, frowned in a warning manner, but Janie blithely ignored them both and shook hands with the departing throng just like she'd earlier greeted them. I'm sure they thought she was part of the family. As a matter of fact, I'm sure the family thought she was part of the family.

"Pleased to meet ya," Steven Bondesky said to Janie. "Sorry about your loss."

"Thank you," she said.

Moving to stand in front of me, my accountant said, "I thought I'd find you here. I need to see you, Huckleberry."

"Let's step outside," I said.

Janie followed us at what for her was a discreet distance. Steven Bondesky can be intimidating.

The day was slowly heating up. Spring was almost over, and summers in Fort Worth are only better than Houston because of the lower humidity, which is to say they're hot but not so wet. But you couldn't prove it by Steven Bondesky, who was already wiping sweat away from his thick, white face. It was the first time I'd ever seen him away from his office. No, come to think of it, he'd been at my father's funeral. It's strange, I thought, the only time I see Steven Bondesky away from his office is at funerals.

I took the initiative. "I want to talk to you, too."

"Yeah? What about?"

"I can't say here." Janie was too close. But I gave him a hint. "You know what you've always said I had and I said I didn't? Well, now I do."

"Oh, you finally found it," he said.

"Shh. You never know who's listening."

"I like that you're careful, Huckleberry. Yeah, come by the office. I'll talk to you there about it. But what I want now is to tell you I got the Plymouth Voyager for you. Jimmy here"—and I was surprised to find the crumpled creep standing at my elbow—"he'll bring it by later, if you're going to be home."

"Sure," I said bravely. Maybe I could get Janie to stay awhile. I knew Steven Hyatt wouldn't be any protection.

"Okay, then." As he lumbered away, his massive frame swaying to and fro from the effort, he growled, "And come see me about the other. I told ya it was there, ya know."

I watched him climb into the rear of a black limo—Jimmy was driving—and as it pulled away from the curb, the next car pulled up. Ralph went around and slid into the passenger seat in front—next to Joaquin!

"Everybody's here," I said.

"Yeah," Janie's face beamed with pure bliss as she

followed my gaze. I had pointed the gardener out to her while he worked in my backyard that very morning. "It's just like in the books," she said.

"So you think we've seen the murderer this morning?" I asked Janie. We were headed for the Malibu, Steven Hyatt supporting us across the uneven pavement of the funeral home parking lot by offering each of us a crooked elbow to hang onto.

"Of course," she said.

"I believe her," said Steven Hyatt.

"Well, it doesn't sound very scientific to me, but if it's true, then which one killed Steven Miller?"

# Twenty-four

We argued about who was Steven Miller's murderer over lunch at the Black-Eyed Pea. Steven Hyatt had us in stitches as he kidded us and made fun of each suspect on our list: "Yeah . . . uh-huh . . . well, it's perfectly clear to me. If Honey didn't do it, then I did!"

"Are you confessing, Steven?" asked Janie, not in the least ruffled by Steven Hyatt's cavalier attitude toward our deductions.

"Sure," he said lightly. "It makes as much sense as your . . . let's see your notes here . . . your Steven Miller, Jr."

"Well," she said defensively, "maybe he didn't want to be a junior all his life."

"Hush, you two," I protested. "Janie, mark that name off your list; that's his daddy we buried today, for crying out loud."

It was only after we had returned home and Steven Hyatt left us to go outside and upstairs to take a nap that Janie and I got down to the real brass tacks.

As she filled me in on her original self-elected assignment to gather details on the laboratory explosion in Florence, I reminded myself to tell her during the next lull in her story what I already knew about Stephen X's involvement with the incident.

"It really is a sophisticated formula, Honey. One that's sure to work. Well, was going to work. No one can find it now. Reckon it must have burned up in the fire and there's no record of it anywhere."

"I just don't understand, Janie. What makes this Italian discovery or invention, or whatever you call it, more likely to work than all the other ones that hit the headlines? Steven Miller told me that someone announces every day that they have the perfect substitute for gasoline, but you don't see us driving around using it, do you?"

"This one was different; not only did it work, but it was cheap to produce and . . ." Janie referred to her notes and read, " '. . . little or no expense to the consumer for conversion to the system.' " She looked up. "That's been the real hang-up on alternate fuel, you know . . . the cost of conversion. It's not that all these scientists couldn't invent one, they just couldn't figure out how to get it to work in the cars and trucks we're driving around in now."

I began to understand. "And this one did?"

"Right. You just pumped it in, and it worked like the good old super unleaded stuff."

"No buying new cars? No extra cost for a doo-hickey for the engine? Just pump it in and drive off?" This was beginning to sound familiar to me, but I couldn't remember why.

"Yeah." She thought she was agreeing with me.

"Sounds too good to be true, doesn't it? Oh, well." And she flipped that part of her notebook closed. "We were probably barking up the wrong tree, anyway, trying to connect something of this magnitude with Steven Miller's death."

"No," I interrupted her and when she looked startled, I realized I had uncharacteristically yelled out the word. I lowered my voice. "What I mean is, what I meant to say is . . ." Good grief, I didn't want to alarm Janie or send her off onto new tangents of thought, but I knew the Italian explosion was connected with Steven Miller's death. Stephen had convinced me of that. But if I told Janie all that I knew . . . "What else did you learn about the Italian thing? Read me the rest of your notes."

Janie seemed dubious, but having gone to the trouble to compile the research, I think she was tickled that I wanted to know about it, even if she didn't now think there was a link between the two events. "Actually, it is interesting. The scientist who died wasn't Italian. Not full-blooded, anyway. He was an American whiz kid in agricultural biology . . . botany . . ." She looked up. "You know what I mean," she said, but went on to explain in her own Janie way. "It's the kind of science that deals with increased grain production, and a better grade of grain, too."

I stretched, trying to act only casually interested in her research. "I understand, but if he was American, what was he doing in Italy?" I added, "Do you want some iced tea?"

"Sure," she replied.

Of course she did, iced tea is the year-round state drink. I headed for the kitchen, and Janie followed, bumping into the dining room table in her single-minded concentration on the notes she read while she walked.

"Here it is," she announced as she joined me in the kitchen. "Arthur Roselli, thirty-eight. Born Hobbs, New Mexico; died . . . well, you know that."

"Arthur?"

Janie looked up. "Pardon?" she said.

"His name is Arthur?"

She checked her notes. "Yes," but she amended her statement by saying, "Was. Was Arthur Roselli. His father was the Italian half; that's why the Roselli. Why? What's wrong with Arthur?"

Not Stephen?

Janie closed the notebook. From memory, she summed up the rest of Arthur Roselli's story. "Invited to participate in international agricultural research exchange . . . four, no, five years ago. Chose Italy because . . . first, his family was from there, and second, because the Italian government gave him a full laboratory for personal research." She paused to thank me as I handed her a glass of tea. "Which," she continued, "we know he did, because he discovered that which he died for . . . and with." Pleased at her report, she smiled and drank her tea.

"Won't someone else be able to figure out his discovery?" I asked.

"Nah, why should they want to? Stuff blew him up, didn't it? Would you want it in your car?"

"I see what you mean," I said. Actually, I saw more than that.

# Twenty-five

Naps are a habit in the South. Always have been. Maybe it's the heat. Probably it's the heat.

Anyway, I wasn't surprised when Janie asked if I minded if she took a small nap before she headed on back to West. It was only a little more than an hour away, but it was going on two-thirty now, and we had eaten a large lunch after a taxing morning.

Anyway, I answered, "Sure," and showed her upstairs.

"My mother's room okay for you?" I asked. "I keep it up."

"Fine," she answered as we turned the curve in the landing. She'd been upstairs already. I never did know why we hadn't a bathroom on the ground floor.

Before entering my mother's small bedroom, she pointed to the middle room and asked, "Now, Honey, what did you say you call that room?"

"The war room."

" 'Cause . . . ?"

"'Cause that's where I do all my planning . . . on where I'm heading next and who I'm going to see when I get there. Oh, yeah, and how I'm going to get there and, of course, what I'm going to wear once I'm there." I indicated the rows of shrouded clothes.

"I'm impressed," she said as she stepped into the room and checked out the tags on the individual bundles. "But doesn't it take an awful lot of time? I mean, what with figuring everything out and sorting it out and then writing it down and all?"

"Maybe so," I replied, "but, Janie, if I don't do all this, I wouldn't know where I'm supposed to be or what I'm supposed to do when I get there. It's just my way of getting organized."

I gently tugged on her arm to get her moving on toward her nap, but nothing would do but she had to inspect my bedroom, too.

"Now, what I don't understand is how all these rooms are the way they are and your room—and the war room—are so . . . different."

I explained as I continued to edge her toward the back bedroom. "The rest of the house? The furniture, the antiques? That's all the aunts' doings. My mother liked it, so they never changed it. Father did add the paneling to his room. And my room? Well, I use it every day. Guess it's just worn out."

Janie continued to ooh and ah as we pulled down the flowered embroidered counterpane on Mother's bed. "This headboard must be eight feet tall, Honey," she said as she measured the distance with her eyes. "And the footboard? What . . . four feet?"

"Think so?" I asked and I left her stretched out on the crisp, cool sheets that I changed whenever my Day-

Timer dictated. *Why, Mother would have died if she ever thought I'd let her room get dusty and stale smelling,* I was thinking as I went back downstairs.

"Honey."

From the bottom of the stairwell, I turned my face upward to see Janie leaning over the top banister. She had dark circles under her eyes and I could tell the excitement of the day had tired her. "Honey," she repeated, "I just thought of something. Do you think we should have gone on out to the cemetery?"

"What makes you think that, Janie?"

"We might have missed him. He might not have gone to the funeral parlor; he might have gone straight to the cemetery."

"No, I think we did just right," I reassured her. She seemed to feel somehow responsible for solving Steven Miller's murder. "Look at all the suspects we've listed."

She nodded and her stocking feet shuffled back into the bedroom. I went on outside, intending to run up to the third floor, but I became distracted when I saw Joaquin and Ralph in the yard, talking and nodding their heads. So, instead of heading up to see Steven Hyatt, I joined them in the back just as Ralph turned to walk away. It might have been my imagination, but I thought Ralph looked halfway angry at something.

"What's wrong with him?" I asked Joaquin, who was kneeling on the ground, staring after the doctor.

He smiled his warm-eyed smile at me. "Guess I'm not moving fast enough for him."

"Oh, come on now," I exclaimed. "How could he think that? You've already done the iris bed and this one." I pointed to the recently tilled rectangular bed

Joaquin had told me was mine to decide what went in it. ‘‘Hey, have you already planted it? I haven't decided yet.’’

‘‘I decided for you.’’ He laughed.

And I decided not to be angry or hurt about it. ‘‘Oh, and what did you plant in such an all-fired hurry?’’ I asked, but laughing as I said it in such a way that Joaquin knew it was all right.

‘‘A little of this and a little of that. You'll see soon enough. Or you'll see some flowers soon,’’ and he pointed to the asymmetrical rows of miniature green plants. ‘‘The seeds will take awhile, but you'll like the results.’’ I could tell he was genuinely pleased with his efforts, and he described what he'd chosen for the new bed. ‘‘It's like an informal English garden,’’ and he went on to say names that meant nothing to me.

As a matter of fact, I was only half listening to him when I heard him say ‘‘. . . and you'll have to lift the burlap up carefully when the ones in this corner have sprouted.’’

‘‘What? Me? What about you?’’

He straightened his back, rubbing it slightly as he arched. He looked tired. ‘‘Sure, I'll do it. I just thought you'd like to know how . . . in case . . .’’

‘‘In case what?’’

‘‘In case Ralph fires me,’’ he said unexpectedly.

‘‘Why should he do that? You're doing a wonderful job.’’

Joaquin took his yard broom from the nearby cart and began sweeping the loose soil on the sidewalk back into the bed. ‘‘I'm only kidding.’’ And he added, ‘‘Doan worry so about et.’’

His lapse into a singsong Spanish accent reminded me

of how accustomed I had become to hearing him speak good English. I persisted, "Ralph seemed okay when you drove him to Steven Miller's funeral today." And then, "Why did you do that, Joaquin? Drive Ralph, I mean? Why didn't he drive himself?"

Like he shouldn't be telling me, like it was something dirty he was going to say, Joaquin bent his head down, and I instinctively stepped in closer and raised my head to hear what I knew were going to be lowered tones. "Ralph's not feelin' so good theese mornin'. He had another round with hees ole lady, and I'ma bettin' she won."

I punched his shoulder. "Stop that," I said. "Speak right," I demanded, infuriated at his behavior. "You don't talk like that."

"Sumtimes, I do," he insisted, laughing as he wheeled his cart down the path toward the clinic garage.

I was so frustrated I wanted to spit in his newly planted garden. The only reason I'd come on out in the yard was to question him about the missing tape cassette, and now I was watching him effortlessly lift the tool-laden cart over the dividing curb between my property and the clinic, and I hadn't confronted him about a thing.

"Wait," I yelled.

"Yes?" Joaquin turned and looked back at me.

I didn't say anything.

"Yes?" he said again and rubbed his hand over the dark hair that hung over his eyes. His dirty hand and sweaty brow connected to leave a grimy palm print on his forehead. I stared at it, fascinated.

Without moving my eyes, I said, "I'm going shopping."

"So?"

"What?"

"So . . . ?" He looked puzzled and stepped back over the curb, moving slowly toward me. "Honey," and his voice sounded far away, although he was coming closer.

I was remembering something . . . but . . . what?

Then it came to me: Joaquin's use of the word so had prodded my memory of how Harry had used that same word . . . with the same inflection. "I think it is rude," I had told Harry. "It sounds like you're saying 'so what,' which also sounds childish, like kids shouting 'ya-ya-yuh-ya-ya' on the playground."

Harry had just laughed and said that in Europe *so* was used to express interest, not derision. Joaquin's use of the word—expressing interest in my shopping trip—caught my ear and reminded me of Harry. I felt so guilty about not calling him . . . but . . .

"Honey," Joaquin said again. He had reached me, and his hands grabbed my arms. "Hey, are you okay?"

"Sure," I answered, pulling away from his grasp, which would have left dirty prints on my upper arms if I hadn't been wearing my dark sweater. "Why?"

"You said you were going shopping . . . and then you just stood there. I thought something was wrong with you."

"No, I'm fine. Oh, a little tired. We all seem to be tired, don't we? I was just going to tell you that I'm going to buy a new tape cassette for my answering machine."

He bent down, looking at my eyes for another second before slewing around toward the parking lot again. "Great," he shouted over his shoulder. "Then you won't miss any phone calls, will you?"

I agreed by weakly nodding my head toward his receding back. I had wanted to seriously confront Joaquin about taking the tape from my machine, but I hadn't pursued the subject. Sighing from my wasted opportunity, I turned toward the house, determined to follow through on at least one intention.

# Twenty-six

Steven Hyatt was awake, dressed in a pair of khaki walking shorts and a cotton shirt that I felt sure had been originally purchased for the Australian outback or "Down Under" as Prusilla and I called it. I giggled.

"So, what's so funny?" he asked.

"Nothing, that is, nothing to do with you. Just remembering a 'friend' of mine. Wondering where she'd got to is all," I finished.

"For a person who has no friends, you seem to have collected a number of friendly nonfriends around you this trip," he said as he led the way back to the beanbag chairs.

As I sank into my chair, I put my finger to my screwed-up lips and replied, "Yes . . . and do you know? I have absolutely no idea how this all came about."

"Well, from what you said last night, it all blew up when you found Steven Miller's body."

"No, it was before then. It was the telephone call. Nothing has been the same since I answered that first telephone call.'' I had told Steven Hyatt about the subsequent calls, and I think I had told him everything else that was going on, but I wasn't sure. Had I told him about the money, I wondered? I was going to have to make out a list like I did with my travel schedule so I'd know to whom I had told what. I'd told Janie about the telephone calls, but not about the money. I'd told Steven Bondesky about the money, but not about the telephone calls. I'd not told Silas Sampson about the telephone calls or the money. I'd told . . .

''Silas Sampson . . .'' And Steven Hyatt paused, ''God . . . what a name. Remind me to put him in one of my movies . . . his name, that is. Where was I? Oh, yes. Silas Sampson thinks the telephone calls and the murder are unrelated, but I think they are.''

''You do?'' I was surprised.

''Yeah. Don't you?''

''Well, yes, I do; but, Steven, I think it has something to do with what you were telling Joaquin last night.''

''About your father's work?'' he asked.

''How did you know that's what I was thinking?''

'' 'Cause it probably struck me about the same time it hit you. Your father was the only other person in this world, the only person besides you and me, who knew about our unknown poets game.''

''Mother,'' I added honestly.

''Honey,'' he said gently, ''your mother never knew the police band was playing past a few months after I met you. She checked out long before we made up the game.''

It hurt to remember, but it was true. Steven Hyatt had been a godsend to Father. His taking me to and picking me up from school had been the only way I could have attended, it never occurring to any of us that I could have ridden the school bus. Father had to stay with Mother, who wandered the house like a pale dust mote blown not by a healthy breeze but by the whisper of a forgotten current gliding through the maze of her understanding.

"She went to bed so early," I remembered. "Then Father would join us for the evening, reading his books and papers. Or working on my . . . toys." I had the grace to blush as I recalled what I had called the models.

"Something else, Steven," I said, "before I forget. Ideas and thoughts have been drifting through my head today like a sieve. Am I crazy or do I vaguely remember Father telling you about an automobile fuel converter for a gasoline substitute?" There, for once today, I'd remembered a complete thought and managed to convey it to someone.

"Yep," he answered. "It was one of the last models he worked on. You know, we showed it to Joaquin last night. Why does that one bother you?"

"Because of something Janie said today." And although I had told Steven Hyatt about Stephen X's explanation of the explosion in Italy, when I related Janie's more simplified account, he understood why it had triggered my remembering another watered-down definition of fuel converters.

Steven Hyatt was excited now. He stood up and started to pace the room. "Okay, let's see what we've got here, besides an implausible plot for a new movie." And he grinned at me, putting me at ease with his jokes, reminding me that, while the subject was serious, he wasn't going to allow it to hurt us, his wit and humor insulating me today just as surely as they had when we were younger.

"Wish I had some paper. I'd graph it out, but since we don't, listen to this. Your father bought the patent to an automobile fuel converter. He often did that, you know. An inventor would come to him—his reputation was tops—and hire him to research an invention . . . or build them a model. Sometimes they just wanted to sell their idea for a little money."

"I remember," I said, remembering.

"Let's say some guy came by with this fuel thing and your father bought it. And then he made this model." Steven Hyatt strode into the next room to look for the one he and Joaquin had examined last night.

He returned with a frown on his face, but it didn't interrupt his train of thought, "I can't find it right now, but let's go ahead and take this a step further, Honey. And say after researching the plans, Mr. Huckleberry decides it's a pretty good invention, one that could really work." He frowned. Steven Hyatt was doing some remembering, himself. "You know, I think I remember him telling me that."

"What?" I exclaimed as excited as he.

"Hush, hush. Let me remember. Now, let's see. I was sitting here and you were sitting there and Mr. H. was . . . I know . . . in that chair, and he said . . ."

I clapped my hand over my mouth so I wouldn't ask any other questions that would distract him.

"He said, 'Steven Hyatt, if I were younger or if Miss Katherine were not so ill, I'd . . . I'd . . .' " He faltered but continued to wave at me to be silent. Finally the words burst through his veil of remembrance and in a theatrical, triumphant pose, he fairly shouted, " 'I'd go in the business myself instead of looking for a buyer. This invention really works.' "

He fell back on the brown beanbag chair. "By George," he muttered.

"By George," I echoed. "Steven, do you think he ever sold it?"

Having solved what he thought was a major part of the problem, Steven Hyatt was casual with his reply. "Nah, he would have sold it to an oil or an automobile company. And if he had—and it really worked like he claimed it did—they would have paid a fortune for it. And we all know, sweet Honey, that your lovely self wouldn't be on the road hustling books for a living if there. . . ."

I *hadn't* told Steven Hyatt about the money.

"Steven . . ." I began.

He wasn't listening, " 'Course that doesn't answer why your Stephen would have found that piece of paper with 'How Far Is It Called to the Grave?' on it. Unless . . . Honey, do you think there is any way you could get Mr. X to give you that piece of paper? It might tell us more than he figured out from reading it."

I forgot about the money for a minute. "Gee, I don't know. You know, I haven't heard from Stephen in two days. Maybe he's given up and gone back to Italy."

"He wouldn't do that without talking to you," Steven Hyatt insisted. "There's got to be a connection between the instructions he found on the arsonist in his laboratory in Florence and the similarity of the inventions."

"But . . ." I protested.

"Honey, this is serious. Your father is somehow connected with the deaths of Steven Miller and that unknown assassin in Italy."

A shiver went up my spine, and I said, "Steven, Father has been dead for ten years."

"Right," he replied, "but it's got to be tied up in that invention. I just feel it, Honey." And he looked closer at me hugging my arms tight around my body to hold off the chill that his words had caused to descend on me. "You feel it, too, don't you?"

"Yes. No. Maybe. I don't know what I feel, Steven. Maybe if I saw the blueprint, I might recognize . . . or feel . . . something from it. I seem to be very good at feeling things. Its something new I've learned about myself. Where did you say the blueprint was?"

"I said I couldn't find it. Or the model. Although I think I remember showing it to Joaquin last night."

I grinned. "Steven Hyatt, you couldn't find your head if you were carrying it in your arms. Let me look."

We went into the smaller room where the stacked blueprints were kept, but after methodically searching for almost a half hour, both of us gave up.

"I know I saw it last night," Steven said.

I didn't answer him because another blueprint had caught my eye. "Steven, look at this one. It looks like . . . no, I'm sure it is . . . look, Steven, it's the blueprint of the house. The one father made when he was remodeling. Building this third floor. Isn't that fascinating?" I used both hands to spread the tightly curled paper onto the table. "Now maybe I can figure out some things that have always bothered me about the house."

"Like what?"

"Like why my nightmares about it always seemed so real. I've found out lately—and I'll tell you about that in a minute—that the house has been hiding some surprises. Maybe there's something else I don't know."

Before he could respond, but right on cue, as if scripted for the imaginary scenario Steven Hyatt claimed he was drafting of our situation, we heard someone call my name from somewhere within the bowels of the house; a thin, reedy cry of "Honey . . . Hon-ney, where are you?"

# Twenty-seven

I glanced quickly at the Timex on my left wrist as I bounded down the outside steps and into the house. I had forgotten about Janie.

She was descending the stairs, rubbing her eyes, which were swollen from her recent sleep. Spotting me at the curve of the landing, she started speaking to me just as if it hadn't been almost two hours since I'd seen her. ''I forget what it's like . . . taking a hard nap in the middle of the day. I feel like someone has been stomping on my head with his boots on. Can I have some more tea, Honey? Hot this time? And then I've got to get on back.'' She looked at the red teapot clock above the kitchen table and said in disgust, ''And I'm going to hit the five o'clock traffic, too.''

''Don't go,'' I said impulsively as I put the filled kettle on the top of the stove.

''What?''

''Stay here with me. Have supper and spend the night. We'll go shopping. There's a few things I want to buy

. . . for the house.'' I kept inventing my argument as I begged her to stay. For some reason, I didn't want be alone in the house tonight. ''I'll wake you up early,'' I said. ''You can open up Pages by ten as usual, if you want to.''

''Well.'' She sipped the hot tea I'd put before her. ''I could call my husband and tell him I'm staying for a sleepover. He won't care.''

''It'll be a good opportunity for me to tell you more about the house . . . about the aunts and all. I know you're interested.''

Janie bargained with me. ''If we go shopping, will you let me help pick out something new for your bedroom?''

''My room?''

''Yes. I was thinking before I went to sleep how nice it would look if you added just a few things. How that old furniture would come alive with the right accessories. And I know just the place to get them.'' She stopped then said, ''I'm sorry, Honey. I do get carried away. What I imagine in your room might be expensive. I shouldn't have said anything.'' She looked embarrassed.

Money?

''Money's no problem,'' I said, surprising myself. At her questioning look, I said, ''That is, I've been thinking about redoing that room, too, and I've put away some . . . a little . . . for redecorating. But I didn't know where to go, and here you are saying you do.'' I took a sip of my own tea, amazed at my audacity. Honey Huckleberry getting ready to throw money away. Just like she had it. Just like it was hers. ''My,'' I added in a weaker voice, ''won't we have fun?''

I washed the teacups while Janie went upstairs to freshen herself, and when I heard her footsteps reach the top stair, I took a deep breath and opened the pantry door. Reaching wildly inside, my outstretched fingers ultimately connected with the spidery string to the light-bulb that, when lit, dimly revealed the interior of the storage area.

It was just as I had left it—lots of gritty debris and lots of stacked hundred dollar bills. I reached under the thin, broken paneling on the floor and withdrew a healthy-sized wad. "Guess I'll see if it's real, anyway," I said to the swaying cord before I pulled it again. The whole operation had taken only seconds, but I felt as winded as if I had run a race. Tomorrow, I vowed, I would have to do something about the money.

Damn, I remembered. I still hadn't told Steven Hyatt about the money.

"Ready?" I jumped. I hadn't heard Janie come back downstairs. My long black skirt hid the cash clenched in my hand, but I was still afraid Janie would see it.

"No, but it won't take me but a minute. Janie, why don't you run upstairs—outside upstairs—and ask Steven Hyatt if he wants to go with us." I'd forgotten about him when I'd asked Janie to stay.

In two shakes of a lamb's tail, I met up with her again right outside my front door. I had run a brush through my hair and a puff over my nose. Other than that, I still looked as I had when we'd gone to Steven Miller's funeral.

"Let's go in my car," I said. "I know Fort Worth, and it'll be easier for me to find wherever it is we're going. Where are we going, anyway?"

The two of us walked toward the clinic—Steven had

politely declined the invitation—and Janie was surprised when I inserted my key and raised one of the basement-level garage doors. But she nodded understandingly as I explained the parking arrangement with the clinic.

It had been a hot day and promised to be an equally warm evening, unusual for this early in the season, but the uncommon heat was promised a wet relief by the roll of thunder in the distance. "It probably won't rain for hours," I told Janie as we roared out of the stuffy garage. "I noticed this morning that my air-conditioning is on the fritz, so you'll have to roll down your window for some fresh air. Sorry about that," I said as she complied, "but it won't be for too much longer. I'm getting a new car . . . today."

Janie looked at me funny. Out of the corner of her eyes.

"Well, I was supposed to get a new car today. A van actually. That Jimmy the Geek you noticed at the funeral this morning? He is or was supposed to bring me a new Plymouth Voyager that my business manager arranged for me." I liked calling Bondesky my business manager. It's funny how your vocabulary changes when a little money comes into your life. It put a whole new perspective on everything. I was dying to tell someone about my newfound wealth. Wish I'd had time to talk to Steven Hyatt before we'd left. Janie had reported that while he'd declined our offer of shopping, he said he'd meet us later for dinner.

As I drove, I glanced sideways at the woman beside me. Janie looked like an aging gnome with a satisfied, pixilated smile on her face. She had called her husband and told him of her nocturnal plans. I'm sure it didn't surprise him. I tried to imagine someone married to this fairy godmother, murder-loving woman. Mr. Janie? I didn't know his name and had forgotten to ask. Actually, I didn't really care. I had money and a girlfriend. I'd never had one before. Just Steven Hyatt. It didn't matter that Janie must be eons older than me. I was used to older people.

Janie's little special place that she wanted to take me shopping turned out to be Laura Ashley for crying out loud. I would never have gone in there alone, but with Janie's support, I braved the wall-to-wall floral patterns, and we strode in side by side like we knew all along that were going up the stairs to the linen department. One of us knew the way.

Actually, once I got past my initial shock of being there, I had to admit I kinda liked it, but Janie went hog-wild. "Pink and green, Honey. Pink and green." That was about all she could say, surrounded by the plethora of colors in clever Victorian designs.

"Pink and green," I told the salesperson, and she chose everything in the shop for me that met that dictate: comforter, sheets, duvet, duvet cover. All, including the curtains, were in a sweet little rose pattern. The towels, however, were striped but, of course, met the requisite color combination. I agreed to buy items that prior to this outing I hadn't known existed.

Janie had the decency to gasp when my personal shopper presented me with the bill.

"Do you take cash?" I asked innocently. "All I have is hundreds."

Celebrating what had been a tense minute for me—the time the salesperson had taken the stack of greenbacks and kept them—Janie and I ordered a double scotch on the rocks at The Original while we waited for

Steven Hyatt to join us. Spending that much money hadn't taken as much time as we had allowed for it.

"I didn't know they delivered," said Janie.

"They didn't know they delivered," I answered. "But thank heavens, we didn't have to carry it all. But what will I do if it comes after you leave? I won't know where everything goes." We had only been together this day, but Janie seemed like my oldest friend. Well, come to think of it, next to Steven Hyatt, she was. Her friendship seemed to complete another gap in my childhood.

"Tell me about the house . . . and the aunts," Janie said.

So I told her about my three maiden, great-aunts. About their lovely home. Why we lived there. Correction: why I lived there amid all the Victorian folderol, real Victorian folderol. We laughed over the aunt's eccentricities. Who was I to laugh? And we sighed over a time gone by.

"Just imagine, Honey," Janie said. "Times were so different back then. A lady could be a real lady," she said, implying that perhaps we weren't.

We ordered the Roosevelt Special—that tells you how old the place is—but I declined another drink. After all, I was driving. But I'd had enough to feel a bit lightheaded when I reached out with one hand to lay it on Janie's arm in a confiding manner. "Do you want to hear the saddest story I've ever heard?" I asked.

"From one of your new books?"

"No, from real life. Oh, don't look so alarmed," I said when I saw her expression. "It's not about me, but it is a story about my family.

"You remember the aunts—Aunt Eddie, Aunt Allie, and Aunt Baby? Well, I told you Aunt Eddie was the oldest, didn't I? Well, she was, but the other two died before she did, which was probably the best way for it to happen 'cause Aunt Eddie always felt so responsible for her sisters. . . .'' My voice trailed off. ''But that's another story.

''The story I want to tell you about is what Aunt Eddie told my mother, right before she died.''

''Before your mother died?'' Janie asked.

''No, Aunt Eddie. She was over ninety—ninety-two, ninety-three, thereabouts—and Father was building the addition on to the house. He knew he had to finish it because he'd started it, but Mother told me that she and Father knew they would probably never live up there on that third floor. That Aunt Eddie was very frail.''

''That is sad,'' Janie agreed.

''Right, but that's not my story, either. One day, Aunt Eddie asked Mother to fix tea for her. She claimed she remembered living in England—before the family moved to America—and she liked a proper tea. Anyway, Mother brought her the teapot—the same one you admired today—and Aunt Eddie said, 'Katherine, did I ever tell you about my gentleman friend?'

''And, of course, Mother said, 'No, Aunt Eddie, you never.' Mother said she was afraid to breathe too loud 'cause if she did, Aunt Eddie might not go on with the tale, but she needn't have worried so; the old woman was already lost in her story.

'' 'My mother . . . your husband Joseph's grandmother . . . was best friends with a woman in New York. That's where we first settled when we emigrated from England. This lady, Mrs. Albert Sims, had also arrived in the United States from Liverpool at the same time my parents and I did, and Sarah Louise—that was Mrs.

Sims's given name—and my mother found solace in one another's company.

" 'After Joseph Huckleberry—he was your Joseph's grandfather—found gainful employment in Fort Worth at the Cotton Exchange, we moved to Texas.' "

"Was that before or after Aunt Allie and Aunt Baby were born? And what about Joseph, Jr.?" Janie wanted to know.

Her interruption disturbed me. In telling Aunt Eddie's story as told to me by my mother, I lost myself in time. I stared at Janie, not recognizing her for a minute, and without answering, I continued in my Aunt Eddie's voice just as I remembered Mother doing when she related it to me.

" 'The two women kept in touch over the years, writing long letters in a beautiful, spidery, black script at least twice a year and, of course, at Christmas. Sarah Louise and her family stayed in New York. New York City, that is. And the women always planned to meet again someday or, better yet, in their letters they began to fantasize about a possible romance between Sarah Louise's oldest son, Marcus, and myself.

" 'I remembered Marcus, although I had been so young when we landed in New York and, like mother, I began to think of him as mine and that the two of us were destined to be together. Of course, Marcus and I never communicated.

" 'When I was twenty-two and had taught at the Fort Worth High School for several years, Mother and Sarah Louise decided it was time Marcus and I got together, so that summer, she and I went to New York City.

" 'The Sims family had prospered and their lifestyle was similar to that of the Huckleberrys' in Texas, a comfortable middle-class environment. Mother and Sarah Louise were ecstatic at being together again, and young Marcus and I were expected to resume our friendship also.

" 'One afternoon, late in our visit, Marcus and I were allowed to go boating alone in Central Park. The day was hot—it was late July—and it did seem cooler on the pond where there were many couples in the small rowboats similar to the one that Marcus had hired. It was such a relief to be away from our mothers and on the cool water. We rowed and talked for several hours.

" 'It was on a Saturday that we went boating. On Monday, Mother and I came back to Texas.' "

The waiter delivered our dinners, cautioning as they always do in Mexican restaurants, "Be careful. Your plate is hot."

When I was younger, I always obeyed the rule and never touched the hot plate. Now, in my newfound independence, I rebelliously readjusted the angle of the "hot" plate before I started to eat. Small gains in autonomy were like giant steps to me. "I hope you like this," I said. "I've been coming here ever since Steven Hyatt brought me on the night we graduated from high school."

Janie looked dumbfounded. "Honey Huckleberry, that's just about the meanest thing I ever heard of anybody doing."

"What?" I asked, but I knew.

"To start a story like that, to get me so caught up in it and all, and then—bang—just stop it cold like that."

"But that's my point, Janie. That's how the story ended. That was my Aunt Eddie's love story. The only one she ever had to tell." I grinned at Janie's reaction.

"I know how you feel. I felt the same way the first time Mother told it to me. Just imagine. Going to New York and rowing around Central Park for two hours was all the romance Aunt Eddie ever had to put in her memory book."

Janie's eyes misted. "That's the saddest story I've ever heard," she agreed.

Although we lingered over coffee, Steven Hyatt never joined us, and finally, about eight o'clock, we headed toward the south side.

As we crossed the parking lot to the house, Janie stumbled and almost fell. She supported herself by leaning heavily on a van parked in the last slot nearest my property. "Damn, Honey, I almost turned my ankle on something."

We both looked down, and in the gathering darkness, I saw a loose pile of stones on the smooth asphalt. "Oh, I know what you stumbled on. That's from Joaquin's wheelbarrow. It must have fallen out when he moved it earlier. Can you walk?"

While Janie rotated her ankle to see if it worked, I thought I heard voices in the yard. Leaving her to struggle with her injury, I peeked around the van. "Oh, my God," I said as I snapped back behind the sheltering vehicle.

"What's wrong?" Janie asked as she simultaneously hobbled to peer over the hood.

I grabbed her by the shirtsleeve and pulled her back. We stood side by side, our rear ends pressing against the metal of the van, as I gasped for the air to give her an explanation. "You know that story I told you about Aunt Eddie?" I asked.

"Yes," she whispered.

"About how sad it was and her not having any life to remember?"

"Yes," she said again.

"Well, I thought about that story all my life and decided I wasn't going to be like Aunt Eddie. When I got old, I wanted to have some memories . . . something more than a sail around a pond. You know what I mean?"

"I think so," she said, but she didn't sound like it. She sounded like she thought I was crazy and if she agreed with me, I'd be sane again. "Honey, what's going on? Who are those people standing in your yard?"

"Well, it's Steven Hyatt. You know him. And Silas Sampson. Did I introduce you at the funeral? And Joaquin. I know you met him. And the other one, the red-haired one? That's *my* Marcus. That's Harry Armstead from South Padre."

"Your love?" Janie was almost as excited as if I had told her Harry was a Mafia hit man. Pulling away from my hold on her sleeve, she stood on tiptoe—the sprained ankle seemingly forgotten—for a better look at him.

"Not exactly. Try lov-er," I said. "I wonder what he's doing here?"

"I think that should be obvious. He's come to see you."

"Not here, he hasn't. He never comes here. I always go there. No,"—and I was emphatic—"not in my house," I said in the same tone that one uses when they read, "Not by the hair on my chinny-chin-chin."

As I came around the van, anger and frustration fueling my steps, I heard all four men say, "Honey!" in such a way that my name seemed to echo in the night.

"Honey," Harry said again, all by himself and with

affection, the way my name was supposed to sound like when it wasn't meaning my name.

"This man claims to know you, Honey," said Silas, acting officious but I imagine secretly delighted that he had a legitimate reason to be asking this stranger what business it was of his to stand there and speak intimately to me.

"Honey," Harry called for the third time, still trying to capture my singular attention. "What's going on? This fellow says he's a copper. He says there's been a murder?"

A murder? It had all happened so long ago in my mind, but by the calendar's count, it had only been five days since I'd left Harry in a parking lot in Brownsville where I think he had been trying to tell me that he loved me.

Before I could answer him, I heard a scream of such proportions that if I hadn't known its source, I would have sworn on a stack of Bibles that it came straight from Hell.

Because I was the closest, I reached her first, so I was the second one to see what had caused Janie to cry out in such fright. She was standing next to the open door of the van where we had hidden to spy out my yard. Her hands were over her now silent mouth, and my eyes followed her wide, fixed stare into the darkened interior.

Jimmy the Geek's eyes were open, too, and I knew that when they closed again, it would be by a coroner's hand, and it would be for the last time. Jimmy was dead, lying in a pool of blood in the backseat of what I now recognized as a new green Plymouth Voyager.

My scream wasn't as loud as Janie's.

# Twenty-eight

I'll admit that what I did involved some risk taking, but I didn't know how else to get a message to Stephen that I needed help. Actually, the only risk was if a policeman called and got the answering machine before someone answered my telephone, because if the receiver wasn't picked up after four rings, you could hear my breathless pleading, "S-t-e-p-h-e-n. I need the original note you found so I can examine it for clues. Please find a way to get it to me." And I told him where to leave it. But at the rate my telephone was being jerked up every time it even looked like it was activated, my worst fear was that Stephen wouldn't get the message either.

I'd found time to slip the new cassette reel into the machine right after we'd all brought Janie in the house when she fainted. I'd thrown wet washrags over the banister at Steven Hyatt and then had run back into my room to insert the tape and record the message before joining them downstairs. It might sound as if I was not sympathetic enough with Janie's predicament, but remember that I knew what happened when you found a body—not the fainting part, but the police part; them coming and going throughout your house, never bothering to tell you what's going on. The thems talking to the theys. By the time I joined them in the living room, Janie had recovered from her swoon, and we could hear sirens in the distance.

In her greatest imagination, fainting would have had to be last on Janie's list of What to Do When You Find the Body. I knew for a fact that she lay awake nights running investigations through her head, trying to make use of all the crime-related information she'd absorbed and stored over the thirty or more years she'd been a mystery fan. Now, here she'd had her big, and probably only, chance of a lifetime, and she'd blown it, screaming and fainting. That's the last thing a pro would want to do upon finding a body.

Janie sat up on my pink couch, supported on either side by Steven Hyatt and Harry while Joaquin and Silas towered over her. They were so solicitous that I wanted to shout out, "Hey, I saw him, too," but instead, I reached through the solid torsos bracketing Janie and patted her knee. She started to cry, and the men dissolved into thin air, so I sat down beside her and took her hand in mine. I knew she was a lot more distraught at how she had reacted than at finding the body.

"I'm so embarrassed," she said in a low voice.

"It's all right," I said.

"It wasn't what I expected," she continued to explain.

"I know," I said.

"No, I mean you plan and plan how you're going to react when you see a victim. How calm and level-headed you're going to be, and then all of a sudden—wham—there's the body, and there you are screaming and fainting."

"I know," I said.

"No, you don't. *You* didn't faint."

"I screamed."

"But you didn't faint."

"Yeah," I said, "but, remember, Janie, this is my second body."

"Oh, yeah," she said and I thought she brightened up just as Silas opened the front door to let in the guys from the black-and-whites and beige and blues and just plain white whites. I've never seen so many police cars in my life.

I pulled on Silas's shoulder and when he bent down I asked him if there had been that many when I'd found Steven Miller.

"Sure. Why?" he'd wanted to know.

"Nothing. Just glad I don't have any neighbors, that's all."

This was still Tuesday. Still the day we'd buried Steven Miller. That meant that I had four more days before I could visit Peggy at the cleaners and tell her that she was right. The guy that came this time—after all Silas was already here—was the right kind of cop. He was short, lean, and ugly, and his burning black eyes didn't miss a trick. Lennox was his name; crime was his game. There was no way anyone was going to lie to this cop about telephone calls or suspects or motives or nothing and get away with it.

"Did you know the deceased?" I heard him ask Janie, and while she was explaining about seeing Jimmy at the funeral that very morning—she'd recovered nicely from the shock of discovering the body—I took the opportunity to tug at Harry's sleeve and pull him toward the kitchen.

Before I could speak to him, he'd gathered me in his arms and given me a big kiss that was not so much comforting as lustful, but one from which I gathered much comfort anyway. I sighed, leaned my head against the collar of his navy cotton jacket for a long beat and then some. I just stood there slumped against him. Finally, knowing our private time together would be at a premium, I asked, "Harry, did I ever tell you hello? And what did you do with Bailey?" I belatedly looked around for the dog. His wet nose pressing against me would be very comforting right now. Like Harry's arms.

"No," he answered. "No, luv, we went straight from eye contact to screams. Honey, can you explain what's going on here? And Bailey is still on the island. With Rosa." I liked that he asked gently, and his composed attitude soothed me enough so that I could quickly explain what he'd inquired about: my return home, Steven Miller, Silas, Steven Hyatt and, of course, Janie Bridges.

"Are any of these Stevens the one you kept mumbling about in Padre?" he asked.

"Oh, no, that's another Steven or Stephen. I didn't mean to keep it all from you, but when I was in Padre, I just didn't think it was going to be so all-fired important. It started with a telephone call that was a mistake, but not really a mistake. I mean it was the right number but for the wrong reason. Then he called again . . ."

"Again!" Silas Sampson was standing in the kitchen doorway. "Honey, you told me you never heard from him again."

Wish I'd kept a log like I'd originally planned. Wish

I'd written down in it who I'd told about Stephen . . . who about the money . . . and whom I'd lied to. And why I'd thought it was important to lie in the first place.

Detective Silas Sampson was all business. "Miss Huckleberry, we need you downtown to answer a few questions. This is Captain Lennox, head of the Investigations Bureau," he said, formally introducing me to his boss. "He'll be questioning you . . . and your friend here," he added, nodding toward Harry.

"Right," I said, looking past his shoulder into Captain Lennox's hard glare. *The buck stops here,* I thought as I picked up my purse and followed them outside where Janie and Steven Hyatt were driving off in an unmarked car. I slapped my palm against my forehead as Harry opened another police car door for me.

"What's the matter?" he whispered.

"Nothing," I told him, but the thought of buck-stopping had reminded of where mucho bucks were just lying around with only a slim sheet of plywood to protect them. I knew I should have done something about the money. I squeezed Harry's hand and looked ahead at Janie and Steven Hyatt's heads bent together in conference in the backseat of the car in front of us. Janie seemed fully recovered and was probably telling Steven Hyatt who'd done Jimmy in. I chuckled. Then suddenly I hit my forehead again.

"Now what?" asked Harry.

This time I answered him. Pulling him over to my side of the backseat, I whispered in his ear, just like Janie was doing in the other car and I wondered if we were asking the same question. "What happened to Joaquin?"

# Twenty-nine

"So what did you tell him?" I asked Janie when we'd contrived through hand and eye signals to wind up in the ladies' room in the police station at the same time.

Knowing I meant Captain Lennox, Janie repeated what she'd told the new man in charge. "I was holding onto my sore ankle with one hand and the door latch of the van with the other when I lost my balance and pitched forward. I didn't fall, but my momentum released the latch and the door swung open. When I straightened up enough to close it, it wouldn't close all the way." She'd overcome her earlier squeamishness to add, "Jimmy's arm had fallen out and was blocking the door," without batting an eye.

"Then I opened the door to see why it wouldn't close and I saw him and I screamed. Then you came, and you saw him, and you screamed. And then . . ."

"Yeah, I know what comes next," I said. "Did Lennox believe you?"

Janie sounded anything but Texan when she answered

with an angry shrug, "So what's not to believe?" She hadn't told any lies and was indignant that her veracity might be in doubt.

*Well, I had lied, and I'd better remember every one of them,* I thought as I hand-combed my hair in the rest room mirror. *Or be prepared to confess. To what? To telling a few lies?*

"You're next, Honey," Janie reminded me, and she didn't mean the line for the stalls.

Before we left the privacy of the room, Janie had a few questions of her own. Like, now, who was Harry? And, sure enough, she and Steven Hyatt were wondering where Joaquin had got to, but, no, she hadn't mentioned him to Lennox. And was I in love with Harry or his dog?

Deciding the famous "best defense" might work for me, I told Lennox as I sat down in his smooth, dark wood visitor's chair, "I think I can clear most of this up for you." He and Silas and the young girl taking notes looked at me in surprise. Lord, lord, where was that correct, reticent young woman of only a week ago?

"We're counting on that, Miss Huckleberry," Lennox replied. "I understand the deceased was coming to see you." He looked down at his notes. "A prearrangement about a vehicle delivery."

"Yes. Well, I assume yes. Jimmy was supposed to be bringing me a Plymouth Voyager, and since we . . . Janie . . . found the Geek in a Plymouth Voyager, I think we can safely assume . . . yes."

"The Geek?"

"Oh, not his name, Captain. Except in my head. I don't know what his real last name is . . . was. But my accountant, Steven Bondesky, can tell you. Jimmy the . . . Jimmy worked for him.''

''We know his real last name,'' Lennox said without saying what it was or how he knew it. ''Miss Huckleberry, Detective Sampson has filled me in on your original complaint. What . . . two weeks ago? The phone calls? From Steven threatening your life?'' Lennox glanced at Silas sitting beside but slightly behind me, ''Now Detective Sampson thinks you might of been holding out on him about some follow-up calls.'' He looked straight at me. ''You shouldn't oughta have done that, Miss Huckleberry. You're going to feel real bad if your keeping mum about the calls led to your friend Steven Miller's death.''

''Yes, I am, Captain, but I still don't think it would have made any difference. Maybe, but I don't think so, but . . .'' and I took a deep breath while offering up a silent prayer that Peggy was right. Lennox looked smart enough. ''That is why I want to tell you everything now. So no one else gets killed.'' They looked more than interested in my next words.

''It all began years ago, and it involves big business and mega money. And the cover-up of a murder in Italy earlier this month.'' I had underestimated my audience. They weren't just interested; they were agog—a word I never thought I'd know the meaning of in my lifetime, but now understood perfectly as I watched the glazed eyes and slack jaws of the professional cops gawking at me. I threw in, ''An illegal alien, a revolutionary invention, an explosion—''

''Miss Huckleberry,'' Lennox interrupted, ''what in the hell are you talking about?''

''I'm talking about telling you everything, helping

you to solve this case, but first,'' I said, standing up and moving toward Lennox's desk, ''first, I have to make a telephone call.''

It says a lot for the quality and predictability of television programming that he just grunted and said, ''Oh, okay,'' and let me do it. *Time out for a commercial break,* I was thinking as I dialed my own number. Who done it, right after this message from our sponsor.

I listened to myself answer my telephone after the fourth ring and immediately punched in my AT&T code for retrieving messages. A tentative ''Honey?'' from the first caller was not surprising when you consider the message I'd left on the machine. It turned out to be one of the executives from a book line I carried, calling from Boston wanting to know why I wasn't at the convention. And then as tentative as his first word, he ended the conversation by asking, ''Honey, are you all right? I mean, if you need me or something, call me.''

The second was a hang-up, but the third told me what I wanted to know.

Hanging up, I turned to Lennox and Silas and said, ''Okay, now we have to go back to my house. The answers are all there.''

So we loaded up again, this time in—would you believe it—the police department's unmarked Plymouth Voyager and headed back toward the south side. Steven Hyatt and Harry had made friends, I was glad to see. They sat together on the backseat of the van, and Janie and I sat in the middle seat. Silas drove and Lennox sat in the passenger seat—you know—the seat where Jimmy had died in that other—the green—Plymouth Voyager. ''They're real comfortable, aren't they?'' I asked no one in particular.

At home, I led the group around to the back of the house. It was way dark by now, and we headed for the gazebo. Entering the little step-up place, I bent over and raised a small flagstone right behind the first latticed wall and picked up the piece of paper I found there.

"Now, let's go in the house," I said, resuming the leadership position toward that goal.

"What the . . ." Captain Lennox swore when he saw the mountain of packages stacked against my front door.

Present drama notwithstanding, Janie and I squealed and said, "They delivered."

The guys brought in the brightly packaged boxes and sacks from Laura Ashley and first sat them on the bottom stair landing on my instructions. "No," I amended, "would y'all mind taking them on up to my room? Then I won't have to later." I looked at Janie, and she nodded her agreement as the four men took the parcels upstairs.

The woman side of us lost the battle to run up and unwrap our new stuff. Instead we made do with "Can you believe we bought so much?" and "Gosh, I hope we still like it."

By the time the men trooped back downstairs, I was sitting in the green chair closest to the red lamp, reading the paper I'd retrieved from the garden.

"So?" said Harry.

"So," I replied firmly, not intimidated by his tone. "So this." And I started right in, not even waiting until they'd all seated themselves. "Seventeen years ago, my father, Joseph Huckleberry, a patent researcher of some renown, was offered a patent from an inventor who didn't have the resources or faith in his discovery to pursue it to its conclusion. Instead, he offered it to my father for a small but decent sum." I'd made up that part, but knowing what an honest man my father was, I was sure it was true. I paused and looked at Steven Hyatt for approval.

He nodded and smiled, and so I went on.

"Father enjoyed making models of the more intriguing inventions that crossed his desk, and this one he particularly liked because he thought it had a good chance of succeeding. It was a fuel converter that was inexpensive to make and easy to install. Combined with one of the experimental formulas—remember this was during the seventies fuel crisis—it had the potential to revolutionize the automotive and oil industries."

"Honey, I don't understand what this—" Silas was becoming restless, but Lennox punched at his sleeve and waved for me to continue.

"My father offered the fuel-converter to two or more of the biggest oil companies. After carefully studying it, they bid against each other, all offering him enormous sums for it." I crossed my fingers and said, "Just how much I don't know, but it was enough so that Father needed a partner to help him to negotiate the price and to represent him at the meetings. You see, my mother was not well during this time." Janie nodded in sympathetic understanding.

"The plans were so good, and the competition for them so earnest that my father had to devise a secret code to communicate with his emissary."

"And he chose 'How Far Is It Called to the Grave?' " Steven Hyatt guessed.

"Yes, Steven. You remember that father sat up there night after night, listening to us rattle on about—oh—everything," and I stopped, looking self-conscious about some of my memories of what we'd discussed. But when he smiled understandingly, I turned to Captain Lennox and asked, ''Do you understand how the game worked?''

''Silas explained it to me,'' he answered. ''Let me get this straight. You think your father used your and Steven Hyatt's little game as the password for a . . . a . . . ?''

When he faltered, searching for the right words, I interjected, ''An international financial agreement?'' A bit dramatic, but I do love dramatic, superlative stories.

Lennox looked dubious but answered, ''Well, if not exactly that, at least a deal important enough to change—''

''But it didn't, though. Change anything, I mean,'' said Harry. ''If it had, why are we still dependent on gasoline and—''

''That's just it,'' Steven Hyatt added, excited at his thought. ''Honey's father sold the blasted thing, but the oil company never used it. They wanted it so no one else could have it.''

''That's not illegal, is it?'' I asked.

''Not that I know of, Miss Huckleberry. Just because you buy something doesn't mean you have to use it. The oil company was just protecting its own interests.''

Janie was indignant. ''But what about the interests of mankind . . . of future generations?'' she sputtered.

''Sod 'em,'' said Harry. ''That's what they would have said, 'cause that's the way they think.'' I smiled at him. Harry understood the them game.

The group was really getting into it now.

It was Silas who brought it back to the original purpose for which we were gathered together in my living room. ''Honey,'' he said, forgetting to call me Miss Huckleberry for the captain's benefit, ''what does all this have to do with the two murders—Steven Miller and Jimmy the . . . well . . . whatever his name is?''

''I'm glad you asked, Silas. And I might can answer you, if you can tell me this: Was there any blood other than Steven Miller's found on my carpet? The night Miller was killed?''

Silas looked surprised. He and Lennox exchanged looks. ''Why, yes, there was. We think it was the killer's. Why? Why do you ask, Honey?''

I smiled, '' 'Cause now I know who killed Steven Miller.''

''And Jimmy the . . . whoever?'' asked Janie.

''Yep,'' I said.

''Who?'' they all asked.

I quit smiling. In fact, I was more than a little sad over my answer. ''Steven Bondesky,'' I said.

# Thirty

Silas was the first to speak. He said, ''You mean the guy we saw at the funeral this morning?'' The fact that it was already the next day's morning seemed irrelevant to him and the rest of the astonished assembly in my living room.

''Bondesky! Your business manager?'' From Janie.

Steven Hyatt knew him as, ''Your accountant?''

And Harry said, ''Who?''

Only Lennox remained calm and professional at my announcement. ''Would you like to explain that remark, Miss Huckleberry?''

''Sure,'' I said.

''As I told you, Father had to have an accomplice—no, wrong choice of words—a negotiator—that's better—to help him with the bargaining. So,''—and I gave the word all its implications—''he used Bondesky.''

''How do you know?'' asked Lennox patiently.

''I suspected, but wasn't sure until I read this note. You saw me pick it up out at the gazebo? Well, sure you did. Anyway, I was thinking that Bondesky was the only other person around who knew my father—besides me and Steven Hyatt.'' Everyone swung their heads around to look at my longtime friend. ''And, of course, he didn't do it,'' I finished emphatically. Some of the eyes that looked upon him weren't so sure that I was right, so I hurried on with my explanation.

''Bondesky knew my father. Father knew the code. The code was used in the mysterious telephone call I received two weeks ago. And I later discovered that the call referred to an explosion and murder in Florence, Italy, one that had to do with alternate fuel.''

''So?'' I couldn't single out any one voice in the chorus of vocal reaction, but I recognized Silas Sampson as he voiced a different and individual criticism of my report. ''Florence, Italy?'' So I turned to address his remark.

''Yes, Florence, Italy. It's a long story, told to me by a friend who is supposedly deceased, but, in fact, is assisting me with this investigation. He is the one who left me the note under the rock since he was the one who took it from the murderer in Italy who was attempting to kill him. My friend's name is Arthur Stephen Roselli. That's Stephen spelled S-t-e-p-h-e-n.''

Lennox persisted with his questioning. ''And this Roselli told you that Bondesky killed Steven Miller?''

''No, Captain. I'm telling you.''

''How do you know Bondesky is the killer?''

''This,'' I said and handed him the piece of old white paper—part of an envelope actually—that I had put in my pocket for the narrative part of my disclosure.

On its creased and dirty surface, my father's handwriting was still visible; a handsome strong script that would have pleased his Aunt Eddie. The words had faded a little but were still very legible. There was the code written on it, just as Stephen had related to me over the telephone, and two smudged telephone numbers. One was mine—had been Father's those many years ago. And the other was, as Stephen had also reported, a number that was no longer in service.

''When Bondesky computerized his accounting system, he had to install a separate line for the modem,'' I told my captive audience. ''He got two new numbers, and this one—the one on the old envelope—was dropped from service. But seventeen years ago, when my Father was alive, it was Steven Bondesky's business telephone number.''

They were awestruck and, at a curt nod from Lennox, Silas moved toward the telephone, then halted when his boss asked, ''But what about the bloodstains? And the murders here in Fort Worth?''

Silas made a move back toward his seat, but Lennox told him, ''No, Sampson, go ahead and put out a pickup on Bondesky. We need to question him anyway. Now, Miss Huckleberry, tell us the rest of your story.'' And his dark eyes demanded the truth—the whole truth.

I told them about Arthur Stephen Roselli, who was supposedly dead but was not. I told them about Steven Miller saying ''Lydia'' before he died. I told them about feeling the blood on Steven Miller's flashlight and wondering later if it had any connection with the dirty bandage Bondesky's assistant had tied around his head. I told them that I thought it did, that I thought Jimmy the Geek had killed Steven Miller.

''Why?'' Captain Lennox asked.

And I told them my first lie of the evening. With my

eyes averted from Lennox, I said, "I don't know." I wasn't going to say, "Because I think they were looking for the probably millions of dollars stashed in my kitchen pantry." Lennox had said the patent deal sounded legal to him, but I wasn't too sure. And then there were taxes and stuff. I'd given them the murderer: let them figure out why.

"Who killed Jimmy then?" Lennox wanted to know.

I shrugged. "Bondesky himself? Maybe, maybe not. They're a lot of strange characters that hang out over there at his office, including not a few policepersons."

"How can I talk to Roselli?" Lennox suddenly wanted to know.

"I'll see if I can arrange that," I answered. "He'll probably be glad to not be dead anymore." And I pushed open the ceiling-high sliding doors that led into the entry hall, walked to the first newel post, and called up the stairs. "Stephen? Do you want to talk to these people? They want to talk to you."

The door to the war room swung slowly open and he came out and started down the steps. "Well done, Honey," said Joaquin.

I responded with, "Thank you, Stephen."

# Thirty-one

''We ought to paint the room first,'' I protested as Janie tore open the Laura Ashley bags, spilling their contents onto the hardwood floor of my bedroom.

She didn't bother to even give me a glance as she unfurled the new sprigged sheets. ''We don't have time. I've gotta be in West in less than two hours. How do you expect me to run a business if I'm all the time involved in chasin' murderers and gettin' pulled in by the cops?'' My crime-loving friend stopped her self-imposed chore of making up my bed with the new linens long enough to gather up the top sheet and hug it to her bosom with a little rigor of delight as she thought of the past two days.

I grabbed half the sheet from her, and together we got it to float over the bed and settle down in perfect folds over the mattress. ''You love it,'' I told her.

''Yeah, I do,'' was her honest answer. ''You know, Honey, all those books I've read on crime—true crime as well as made-up mysteries? Well, there're nothing like the real thing. Now, don't get me wrong, I'm sorry the people are dead. Steven Miller and Jimmy . . . what did Lennox say his last name was?'' She struggled to fit the new down comforter into a blooming duvet cover.

''I didn't kill them. Wouldn't have killed them. Couldn't have killed them. But, now that they are dead, I'm glad I could be of some help in solving their murders.'' She smoothed a matching sham before stuffing it full of pillow. ''I did, didn't I? Help you? I mean, you figured it out, but I meant to ask you last night—sorry I conked out on you like that, but I was so tired—how did you know Joaquin was Stephen? I understand about the Bondesky role, but not about Joaquin.''

''Little things,'' I answered. ''He had a European, not Californian, feel about him for one, and then, too, I didn't have any instinctive fear toward him. So when I knew that he had taken the tape, I tried to figure out a positive reason. And getting rid of the accidentally taped conversation was all I could come up with.''

We were still opening bags and ripping price tags off towels while I tried to verbalize the reasons I had correctly pegged Joaquin as the mysterious Stephen X. ''Oh, and the blueprint and the model for the fuel converter is missing from my Father's collection. Since Steven Hyatt and I saw it only—when was it? Night before last? We guessed that Joaquin had taken it.''

We'd about finished unpacking the new stuff and I ran downstairs to get a plastic garbage bag to stuff the empty sacks into. Janie folded hers carefully before jamming them into the bag. She was uncharacteristically quiet as we worked to clean up the mess the new purchases had made. She seemed to be thinking and finally, she said, ''There's got to be more to it than that.''

"Well, yeah, I guess there is. You see, Janie, the message I left on the machine? Before we went to the police station? Well, I told Stephen X to leave the note where I used to sing with my parents, that he'd remember where that was, and he did."

"And that was where? Honestly, Honey." Janie wanted me to dot the i's.

"The gazebo out back. The only person I'd told that story to was Joaquin. On Saturday night. That was the clincher. When I called from the police station to get my messages, his said, 'Okay, I understand.' I prayed all the time I was taking y'all out to the gazebo that it would be there, and when it was, well, that was that. Stephen had to be Joaquin."

"I gotta go. I gotta open Pages."

"Why? You're the owner. What difference will it make if you're a few minutes late? Or your husband can open the bookstore."

"Him," she said without emotion, leaving me to again wonder about her husband.

"Leave the curtains," I said as she tried to hold them up to one of the windows. "I'll get Ralph to find someone to hang them."

She put the curtains on the window seat, and we stood back to look at the little miracle we'd wrought. Spring might be slow starting this year in Fort Worth, but it was a blooming greenhouse in my bedroom. Pink and green . . . I should say so.

"Do you like it?" Janie asked in a funny voice.

"It scares me, but, yes, I do. I think so, anyway." We started down the stairs, me dragging the wastepaper-stuffed garbage bag. "Stop long enough for coffee before you go," I entreated. "And you can fix it in that percolator you like. Reckon I'll have to learn, 'cause instant won't ever taste the same to me again.''

''All right,'' she agreed. ''But just long enough for you to tell me about the dead man we found in the van.''

''Plymouth Voyager. It's called a Plymouth Voyager, and I think it's mine, but I'll have to check that out with Bondesky.''

We were suddenly quiet, thinking of the man who had been arrested last night.

''Wonder why?'' Janie asked.

I sat down at the kitchen table as she ran the water for the coffee. ''I don't know, but I bet I find out today.''

''Have you talked to Joaquin?''

''No, I went to bed right after you did. Right after he went off with Lennox and Silas.''

''Was it any fun for you, Honey, being involved in such a mess and having to come up with the answers?''

''Well, I didn't get the same thrill that you did. Solving murders that happen in my living room—and parking lot—are not my cup of tea as they are yours. But, yeah, there's a part of me that says, 'My, wasn't that exciting.' '' I hurried to add, ''But not enough so that I want to do it again . . . anytime soon.''

Coffee didn't take long, and a little after nine, Janie took a long last look around the living room, sighed, and gathered her things together. I tried to get her to take the nightgown and slippers I'd bought her the day before, but she patted my hand and said, ''No, put them in that chest of drawers in your mother's room. That way they'll be there when I come again. If you ever want me to come again?''

Telling her not to be silly, we walked arm-in-arm to her car still parked under the only remaining oak tree in front. I thanked her again for . . . for everything. And she thanked me for the same. And finally, with one last good-bye wave, she was off around the corner and gone. I walked back toward the house, counting in my mind how many other good-byes I'd have to make that day.

# Thirty-two

Harry was waiting for me in the gazebo. I had seen him when I'd looked out of the upstairs window of the war room. He was sitting and staring at the roses in my garden, mesmerized just like he'd get when he was watching the waves back home.

I thought of Aunt Eddie as I went down to greet him. How she never got to look out her window to see a man who loved her waiting for her in a flower garden, and so when I got to him, I had a little half smile on my lips. "Harry," I said softly.

And when I went into his arms, I felt safe and secure just like a ship docking at its home berth.

"I love you," he said into the top of my hair, and this time I heard him.

I don't cry often—in fact, can't remember the last time—but I cried when Harry whispered his love into my hair.

"Hush, hush," he crooned as he cradled me in his

arms and rocked us both in a swaying motion. ''It's all over now.''

When I pulled back and looked at him, I saw the sea. Saw it in his eyes. Saw the shoreline and the waves coming in like I was standing on the last existing sand dune on South Padre Island. Saw the wave and felt its spray. Smelled its tangy fragrance and tasted its salty flavor. And once again, I recognized the sanctuary it offered.

But when I looked up to gaze at the Gulf clouds, my eyes left his and all I saw was the house watching us there in the garden.

I shivered.

''Come back with me now,'' he said, his first words reflecting the withdrawal he sensed in me.

''Harry, what are you doing here?'' Those were the words I should have asked him last night.

''I came to get down on my knees, to beg you to marry me.'' He grinned. ''Lord, luv, I didn't know . . .'' His head indicated the house. ''I never knew.'' He added another half sentence, ''No wonder . . .''

''And now? Now, do you still love me? Still want me?''

''More than ever, Honey. I have to have you now. It's my duty and my pleasure to take you away from all this now.''

And Harry got down on his knees on that spring morning whose soft breezes were blowing right up from the southern coast that gave him his life's breath. ''Honey,'' he said, ''every time you came to the island, I loved you a little more. And then . . . finally, this last time, I knew I couldn't let you go, but I did. When I got home—back from Brownsville—I knew I'd made a mistake not settling anything between us.''

His red head bent over my hand. ''I had to come. Had to say it out loud and hear your answer. I hope it's yes, Honey. Honey, will you marry me? I love you so.''

What a pretty portrait we must have made there in the garden. I don't believe in ghosts—never have—but wouldn't Aunt Eddie have loved it. What would Aunt Eddie have done? I glanced up from Harry's red hair and glanced up at the window of the war room. What did we look like from there? Then I turned my head and looked at the steel, weatherproofed windows of the clinic. Catching a movement from one of the windows. Ralph's? I pulled away from Harry.

''Honey?'' Harry stood up.

''That's the most wonderful thing anyone has ever said to me,'' I told him. ''And, Harry, I love you, too.''

''But . . . ?''

''But, I don't know.'' I ran my fingers through my hair. ''So much has happened. I have such responsibilities.''

He reached out and pulled me back into his arms and his kiss was like a silent echo of his words, like he could convince me with passion. And it might have worked if the house hadn't still been watching us.

''Maybe'' was all I could give him, and we walked back to the house to get his bag from where he'd left it when he'd spent the night with Steven Hyatt.

Steven was leaving, too.

''Made a call to New York, and I've got a lead on how to get out from under this mess.'' His thin face beamed and then clouded over. ''At least, I think I do.''

It was decided that Steven would drive Harry to the

airport in Steven's rental car. "I like him, Honey," Steven Hyatt whispered to me. "Don't let him get away."

We were going down the outside steps to the car when I had a sudden thought. "Wait. Wait. Both of you. I'll be right back."

I ran into the house and straight to the kitchen, where I scrounged around in the trash and came up with one of the discarded Laura Ashley bags. Opening the pantry door, I kicked the plywood off the money hidden underneath and scooped up the hastily counted bundles into the sack. When the floor was cleared, I covered the currency with layers of pale pink tissue paper.

I dashed back to the car. "Here," I said to Steven Hyatt. "I want you to have this."

"You bought me something at Laura Ashley?" he asked, his eyes showing amusement.

"No, I just used their bag, that's all."

"Well, what is it, Honey?" And he made like he was going to open it.

I grabbed his arm. "No! I mean, no, don't open it here." Inspiration hit me. "It's something of my father's that I want you to have. Something that he would have wanted you to have, if he'd thought of it. Promise me, Steven Hyatt, that you won't let it out of your sight on the plane and that you won't open it until you get in New York."

New York! Was I crazy?

"No, not New York. Well, yes, I mean New York, but not in the airport. In your hotel room. Yes, promise me you won't open it until you are alone in your hotel room in New York City." In my imagination, I could visualize what would happen if Steven Hyatt began pulling hundred dollar bills, the equivalent of about twenty Plymouth Voyagers, out of a shopping bag in the middle of Kennedy Airport in New York.

"Calm down, Honey," he soothed. "I promise." He took the bag. "It's heavy."

"No, not really," I answered as he shifted the bag's strings to his left hand while his right gathered me into a quick embrace.

And they were gone.

As I walked through the silent house, even the familiar creaks in the carpet-covered hardwood floors reverberated louder than I remembered. I cleared my throat and the sound from my own mouth sounded eerie. I shivered as I had earlier in the gazebo. Only Harry wasn't there to take away the cold chill. I had sent him away, and now I was wondering just how big a mistake that had been.

Used to being alone, I was surprised that I felt lonely.

I ran my fingers along the polished surface of the dining room table. Now my memories were not of how my father had looked, his face dead upon the table, but of the scene the table had reflected from the sparkling light of the high chandelier when we had all gathered around it to have coffee and kolaches the morning before.

We had laughed and . . . Who had been there?

Janie, I knew. Steven Hyatt and, oh yes . . . Silas.

That's what I would do. I'd call Silas and ask . . . ask about Steven Bondesky.

That's what I would do.

# Thirty-three

I didn't know him.

I had seen him just yesterday at Steven Miller's funeral, and today I didn't know him.

Steven Bondesky looked gray and old and less substantial than I remembered. Even though he had seemed out of place at the funeral, he had still looked like himself: big, blustery, and slightly rude.

The old man the guard led into the spare interrogation room at the city jail wasn't anyone I knew.

Until he spoke.

The audacious, raspy voice was the same.

"So, Huckleberry. You wanted to see me?" His eyes didn't quite meet mine.

"How are you, Bondesky?"

"So, how's there to be? I'm in jail. And I hear that you're the one that fingered me. The one who put me here." He raised his brown eyes to mine, and there was disbelief in them, "Is it true?"

"That I told them you and my father must have been

partners? That the telephone number on the envelope was your old business number? That I wondered if you had been the one to kill Jimmy?'' I returned his stare. ''Yes, I'm the one.''

''Ahhh!'' and his exclamation startled me. It sounded like a wounded animal.

''Bondesky, was I wrong? I'll do anything in the world for you. Help you any way I can, if you tell me I was wrong.''

He wiped one of his beefsteak-sized hands across his eyes and said, ''Nah, you were right.'' Then he hurried to add, ''About your father and me; not Jimmy though. No, not about my Jimmy.''

''Tell me about it. Please, tell me all about it . . . and the money. Don't forget about the money.''

He looked more like the old Bondesky when he shifted his eyes around the narrow room where Silas had arranged for us to meet and whispered in a croaking voice, ''Shh, Huckleberry. Don't mention that stuff. That's not a part of this.''

''Then what is, Bondesky?''

Louder, he said, ''Your father and I pulled off a good one. Back then. I set it all up, of course. Your father didn't know how, wouldn't have even known to do it, much less how. I convinced him that it was for you.''

''Me?''

''Yeah, you know how crazy he was about you.'' It was a statement, not a question. ''Always coming in and telling me about you . . . and then that kid . . . that Steven Hyatt.''

''All the money Joseph had put aside for you didn't amount to much.'' He amended his statement. ''Well, some, I guess. That's what you've been living on up to now. He had enough money to send you to college, and then there was the house—free and clear. He was proud of leaving that for you.''

''I know. I know about that part. But what about the other?'' I gazed about the room as suspicious of hidden ears as Bondesky.

''He came to me. Excited like . . . because he had found this crazy invention that could maybe rock the world. After he explained it to me, I got to figuring the angles. Convinced him that he could sell it to one of the oil companies for more money than he'd ever get from trying to make it work himself.'' He paused to remind me, ''You know, Huckleberry, your father with all his smarts wasn't much good at some things. He would never have made it on his own, no matter how good the thing was. He didn't have that cutthroat edge it takes to make some things happen.''

I nodded my agreement and, satisfied that I understood, he went on. ''It worked like a charm. I made a few calls, and then the ball started rolling. All kinds of characters began coming out of the woodwork. It scared your father, and so that's when we come up with the idea of the code. It was my idea to use the poem,'' he said proudly. ''The 'How Far Is It Called from the Grave' one. I knew it was your favorite.''

''How . . . how?''

''From your father. Told you that Joseph used to talk a lot to me about you. Even know what your secret name is.''

''Lydia,'' I whispered.

That's when I found out that the Steven Bondesky I had imagined in my youth was the real one after all. The brute with the heart of gold that I visualized when Father and I had visited him in his garagelike office over on the west side.

Unbelievably, his voice softened. ''Yeah, me and Jimmy always called you that when we talked about you.''

I was incredulous. ''Jimmy?'' I asked faintly.

''Jimmy was like my son. I've taken care of him ever since he came back from Nam. He was all right, just a little upset ever since then. You can't blame him,'' he added defensively. ''He came back not right, and there was no one else to help him. Just me. And we both loved you.'' The big man's eyes filled, and I turned away. I didn't have the courage to watch Steven Bondesky cry.

''Aw, Huckleberry, why did they have to go and kill my Jimmy? He wasn't bad. He never hurt nobody. He just watched out for you and the house. He was always watching the house for you.''

''His ear?'' I asked.

''Wasn't anything wrong with his ear. He wore that bandage or one like it, whenever I could get him to change it, ever since he came back to the States. It was part of his war troubles. The part that was all in his head.''

I had more questions. ''Stephen? No, I mean Roselli? How did he fit in this?''

''It had been on the news. About his fuel breakthrough. And I remembered what your father and I did before with the first invention. So, I thought I could make a little more money for you. It worried me that you hadn't ever found the other money, and I thought maybe it had been stolen. But I couldn't ask you about it because I had promised your father. Where was it, anyway? Where'd you finally find it?''

"Under the stairs," I said, and told him about the pantry.

"But what about this new invention, or rather, formula? What did you do, Bondesky?"

"I made a few phone calls. To some of the old numbers I had from before. And everything seemed to be going okay, but then everything went wrong. They wanted to destroy the invention this time, not just buy it from the inventor. Well, okay, I said. I'll set it up. Honest, Huckleberry, I was the one who was scared this time. These new guys don't play by the same rules."

Bondesky went on to tell me how he'd insisted they use the old code—the poem—to keep in contact. Had even given them the original envelope to make sure they remembered it. And he'd insisted that no one get hurt.

"But they weren't like the old contacts," he repeated. "I think maybe they're big boys." He looked around carefully now, mindful of more than police bugs. "I think they were Mafia."

"No," I exclaimed.

"By the time I realized what was going on, it was too late. That's why I sent Jimmy to watch out for you. And I'm sorry about the van, Huckleberry. I'll send a new one out to you tomorrow."

"What are you talking about, Bondesky? You're in jail. You might not have actually killed anyone, but you're still in trouble about the explosion in Florence. I mean, you didn't do it, but you knew about it. Oh, not the explosion, but about the . . . the . . . the deal. I'm sure they won't let you get away with that. And . . . how can you get me another van? You're in jail," I repeated.

For the first time, I thought I saw a spark of the crafty old accountant I knew and now understood was all right to love. He motioned me forward and we bent our heads over the scarred table between us. ‘‘Remember the cops that always hung out at my shop? Well, it ain’t really so bad in here. I know most of the guards, and they’ve said they’d help me out with anything I needed. Short of getting me out, of course. They know by now that I didn’t kill Jimmy, but they think they might have me on some business angles. I’ll be out soon.’’ I think he laughed, but since I’d never heard him do so, I couldn’t be sure.

‘‘You better go now, Huckleberry.’’ And then, like he had to say it at least once, he added in a very un-Bondesky-like voice, ‘‘Lydia.’’

Tears suddenly stung the insides of my eyes, and I stood and clutched my purse. I turned blindly toward the door but stopped suddenly as I remembered one more thing I wanted to ask him.

‘‘Steven Miller. How can you be so sure that Jimmy didn’t kill Steven Miller?’’

They were true Bondesky eyes again as they narrowed in the broad face wet with a fine sheen of angry sweat. ‘‘Trust me. I know. What I don’t know is who did kill Miller. I don’t know. I don’t know—yet. But I will.’’ He stood up, filling the tiny room with his bulk. ‘‘I’ll tell you this, Huckleberry, I think Jimmy knew. I think Jimmy knew who killed Steven Miller.’’

# Thirty-four

I drove down by the front of my house before circling to put the Malibu in the clinic's garage. What I saw on my front porch surprised me. Leaning against the white column by the top step, looking for all the world like the packages delivered the night before, was Joaquin.

As I hurried around from the back, I remembered that I couldn't call him that anymore. He was Stephen . . . no, not Stephen . . . oh, what was his name? Roselli. Arthur. "Arthur, Arthur," I muttered under my breath as I hurried up the steps, but, "Joaquin!" was what I said when I saw his tired body slumped against the post.

"Joaquin! What on earth has happened to you?"

He must have been half asleep, because he raised heavy eyelids to look at me, and he didn't seem to be able to focus. There were dark shadows under his eyes, and his normally tanned complexion looked like old clay smudged with dirt along his jawline.

"Honey, I've been waiting for you." It seemed to take all his effort to talk.

''I've been at the jail,'' I said.

''Me, too. All night.''

I felt guilty. I should have asked Silas or somebody about Joaquin. I could have given him a ride home. Home? Was this home anymore?

''I need your help,'' he said.

''What? What can I do?''

''Do you have a key to the clinic?'' he asked.

''A key to the . . . ? Of course, this is Wednesday. They close at noon on Wednesday. Don't you have a key? Didn't Ralph give you one?''

''Yes, but I must have put it in another pocket. My sweater maybe. Anyway, it's locked up inside, and there's no one there.''

He looked so exhausted as if even talking to me was wearing him out.

''No, I don't have one. No reason for me to. But Joaquin, you've got to rest. You're about to fall over here on my porch. I know. You can sleep upstairs. Steven Hyatt and Harry are gone, and there'll be plenty of peace and quiet.'' I guided his unprotesting body down the steps and around to the side of the house.

''There's a shower upstairs—a small one, but if you can wait to take one before you fall down dead, you'll feel better. I'll get you some fresh towels from the house.''

''Don't bother, Honey. I'm too tired.''

I assured him that it was no bother, and after discovering that he hadn't eaten anything but donuts since he'd left with the police last night, I scurried around the kitchen whipping up my specialty, tuna fish on toast.

Having heard the water running as I stirred in the mayo, I knew that he'd followed my advice, and so I wasn't surprised when he opened the door at the top of the stairs dressed in one of Steven Hyatt's old terry robes. His thick, black hair was still wet, and drops of water glistened in his mustache. He gratefully took the dry towels I offered him.

Joaquin tried to talk, to tell me everything that had happened at the police station, but it was hard to do with his mouth full. He offered me the last half of the last sandwich on the plate, but I waved it away, and he stuffed it in his mouth, devouring it in two bites. I did, however, join him for a cup of red wine that we'd found in Steven Hyatt's cooler, still cold in neck-deep melted ice.

"Steven Hyatt never did clean up his messes," I said as I looked around the cluttered room. There were still blankets on the couch, and some on the floor, where I guessed Harry had slept. I wouldn't have invited Harry to spend the night with me even if the two of us had been alone. Not in the house. Not in Aunt Eddie's house.

"I don't mind the mess, Honey. I'm one myself." He yawned as he leaned back into the pillows on the couch. "You were right. I do feel better now."

"Good, 'cause I want to know . . ."

What I wanted to know would have to wait. Arthur Stephen Roselli—a.k.a. Joaquin Verde—was sound asleep in Stephen Hyatt's swaddle of sheets and blankets. His complexion was ruddier now. Actually, it was a little flushed, and motherly like, I touched his cheek for fever as I covered him with a quilt I found on the floor. He was all right, I decided. Just overtired.

I wandered around the room, strangely reluctant to leave. It was like I was forgetting to do something. Roaming into the side room, I saw the blueprint of the house I had left on the table. It was still tightly curled like it was holding fast to its mysteries. I picked it up and took it downstairs with me, leaving Joaquin to his much-needed rest.

I had work to do.

Joaquin almost slept the clock around.

The telephone didn't wake him; I raced to catch it every time it rang—before the answering machine did—so I usually caught it on the first ring unless I was deep in the pantry.

Harry called, of course, and we finally had the good long talk we'd needed to have. It was a shame that the only privacy we could find was to be five hundred miles away from each other.

And Janie's call was predictable. "What's happening? Who did it? Is anybody else dead?"

But Steven Hyatt's was a delight. "Honey, my God. Honey, my God, where did you get it? Is it real? What do you want me to do with it? Honey, my God."

Assuring him the money was indeed legal tender and legal for me to have—Lennox had assured me of that—he relaxed, but he still wanted to know why I had given it to him.

"It's from me and father," I told him. "For your debts so you won't have to play tag with the Mafia anymore. They're trouble, Steven. Just ask Bondesky."

"For God's sake, Honey, I can't take your money."

"Of course, you can. No, wait, I know. Use it for an investment for me. That's it. I don't have any investments and, Steven, you know I trust your talent. This next project—the Australian one—is going to be a big success. I just feel it. And I want a piece of the action.

That's how you say it, don't you? Let me be your angel.'' That sounded right.

''You are my angel, Honey.'' He sounded frustrated. ''Oh, all right, but I hope you know what you are asking of me. I know I can't ignore your feelings. Now I'll have to make it . . . and make it big, so I won't let you down. That's a dirty thing to do to me, Honey.''

Before we hung up, I added, ''And if that's not enough, if you need any more . . .''

''More! There's more? Honey, how much is there, and where did you say you found it?''

It was typical of Steven Hyatt not to ask any more questions, and while most of the time it annoyed me, today I was glad that he was behaving normally for him. He obviously was too overwhelmed with the money and prospect of freedom from the mob to be more concerned with the source of the pink-tissue wrapped packages he'd unloaded in his hotel room.

And I was relieved, because overwhelmed myself, I might have told him that the Laura Ashley shopping bag he'd carried innocently into New York City was only a drop in the bucket to the mounds of cash that between telephone calls I'd eventually pulled from the fake insulation behind the stairs.

My cup runneth over.

At least my kitchen did. There was money everywhere. Maybe, I thought halfway into my treasure hunt, maybe I should have left it right where it was, but it was like eating peanuts. One just won't do, and you keep on until the bowl is empty. Only the bowl—kitchen in this case—just kept getting fuller. It was hell having all that money and no place to put it. I must have dragged it to about every possible hiding place in the house before I finally decided to stuff it into the top of the upright piano. Even then it almost didn't fit.

I had just closed the top of the piano when I heard Joaquin on the stairs. Looking around for any stray hundreds—they were slippery things—I ran to the front door to let him in before he rang the doorbell.

He was still wearing his old grungies that he'd had on the day before—actually two days now—but he looked clean himself and refreshed.

I was surprised at his first words. "I've seen you like this before. Tell me, Honey, is this a fetish of some kind?"

"I don't understand."

"No? Then I suggest you go take a look in the mirror." He followed me into the house. I ran into the living room to look at myself in the mirror over the mantel. "I know, don't tell me, when you're alone in the house, you dress up like this. Why? To keep the goblins away or to keep them company? Which?"

"The pantry," I said weakly, gazing at my reflection and recognizing the physical destruction I'd forgotten the little room could wreak upon me. "I've been busy all morning."

"Ah, yes. That's where I remember you collect these lovely cobwebs," and he pulled one out of my hair, its dusty strings stretching between us. "Honey, I told you I'd clean it out for you."

And we both stopped at that.

Joaquin might have cleaned out my pantry, but Arthur Stephen Roselli?

There was an instant awkwardness that our previous banter couldn't erase. "We've got to talk," we both said at the same time.

"But not now," he added. "I promised the police I'd come back to the station today, and I've just got time to change clothes at the clinic and make it there. Honey, I'm embarrassed, but I have one more favor to ask of you. May I borrow your car? I won't be long, I promise." He gently brushed some more cobwebs away from my face. "And then we'll talk. I'll tell you everything I know about what's been going on. I know, I'll take you to dinner."

"I'd like that," I said still shy at this new Joaquin. Maybe I'd find out who this man really was. The phantom phone caller or the congenial gardener? Or maybe someone else entirely. "I'll be ready."

He broke the strain between us with his next words. "Oh, and while we won't go to someplace all that fancy, I do think something black would go with your atmospheric attire, and I do have to mention, I don't think spiders are in this season."

I swatted at a dead spider I had just noticed on my forearm.

He was laughing as he went out the front door and still laughing as he made a clean military turn back. "The keys? And this; I found it in your mailbox." We exchanged items. I gave him the keys to the Malibu, and he gave me a manila envelope in which—after he left again—I found another set of keys and a bill of sale stating, "Jay Owen Plymouth has received payment in full from Miss Honey Huckleberry for one Plymouth Voyager."

Excited, I ran out of the house and finally located the new van in the back parking lot. Exactly where the green one had been parked on Tuesday night. The one with Jimmy's body in it.

I was afraid to open it.

"Honey, how are you? Jesus, you look a fright." Ralph's silent approach startled me.

"Ralph. I'm so glad to see you. Will you do me a big favor? Will you open up this van for me?"

"Why are you so dirty?" he asked fascinated by my appearance.

"Oh, never mind that. I've just been doing some deep housekeeping, that's all. It'll wash off, it always does. I don't think I've ever cleaned like I have today, but it feels good. Before I'm through, I'm going to sweep the cobwebs out of every corner of the house. Every corner I can find. I swear, Ralph, if you could see what's hidden around in that house . . . but would you . . . would you open the van for me?"

"Of course, Honey," he said, still looking at me strangely. "But there're no dead bodies in this one."

"I hope you're right, Ralph," I said as he took the keys and deftly unlocked the doors to reveal the shiny new navy interior. Warm waves of new car smell wafted over us as we peered inside.

"See," he said, "there's nothing to be afraid of now, Honey."

# Thirty-five

"I'm going to be leaving tomorrow, Honey," Joaquin said as we finished our after-dinner coffee at Joe T. Garcia's.

I'd told him he had to say he'd eaten at the north side Mexican restaurant or no one would believe him when he'd said he'd been in Fort Worth. Actually, the purple skirt and embroidered white Mexican blouse were all I could find in the war room that I felt like wearing that night, so the leaning, ramshackle restaurant seemed appropriate. The night was cool enough for me to pull the bright, flowered shawl around my shoulders, but warm enough for us to eat out on the patio. The waiters rushed about delivering trays of monster-sized margueritas to other diners, managing to dodge the strolling guitarist, and not spilling the drinks into the fountain that our waiter assured us had been just turned on for the first time this spring.

I turned back from the festive sight to make sure I'd heard him correctly. "You're leaving tomorrow? What about the police? Won't they need you to testify or something?'' I was suddenly disconcerted to know that Joaquin was going to disappear from my life.

He reached across our table to cover my hand with his. His hand was large and rough, from the gardening work I supposed, but probably rough before that, too. As an agriculturist, he'd told me, he'd spent a lot of time in the fields. When his hand warmed mine, I realized just how cool the evening had become. ''I'm going to trust you, Honey. Because I think I can. Yes, to answer your question, the police, the FBI and, I think, the CIA, have warned me to stay for awhile, but I've got to get back to Italy. Quickly.''

''But how?''

''The same way I came in . . . through Canada. There are too many questions the officials want to know that I'm not prepared to answer. Not right now, not to them.''

''Like what?''

''Like they should be asking me about the explosion at my lab, but instead, I'm getting more questions about my formula. Especially, from a couple of guys no one has properly identified yet.'' He took his hand away, and I felt cold. He folded his hands together and locked them under his chin, his elbows on the table, as he spoke. ''I have been told more mystery interrogators will show up tomorrow. I've got to get away first.''

I was not familiar with the intensity of his words, but then with what was I really familiar with—this new Joaquin . . . Stephen?

We'd talked about our first telephone calls. How and why we'd come to trust each other. Me, out of instinct, and him, out of desperation. "I had no other way. I didn't mean to terrorize you."

He'd come home from downtown exhausted again, but insisting that we carry out our plans for dinner. I had been ready to demur, because although I was bathed and dressed for the outing, I, too, was tired. The job I had finished after Joaquin left for the police station—one I had put off until its accompanying noise wouldn't wake him—had depleted my energy. But both of us had revived with the cheerful atmosphere of the Mexican restaurant. Now the golden lights strung across the patio seemed too garish and the musical gaiety surrounding us too forced.

Death and intrigue had crept their way back into our evening.

Joaquin saw me pulling the shawl tightly around my arms, and he turned to signal the waiter. "We'd better go," he said.

"Wait, Joaquin. Who's coming tomorrow? Who'd they say?"

"A couple of men from Italy. Along with one of my fellow scientists. And I don't want to be here to greet them."

"Why?" I questioned. "Why not, Joaquin?"

He stood over me, reaching for my hand, and when I looked up, he looked dark and foreboding against the backdrop of the festooned patio. "You still don't really understand how big this is, do you, Honey?"

I didn't answer him, and we were quiet on the way back to the south side. Joaquin drove the Malibu; I wasn't ready to tackle the Voyager yet. *What's not to understand?* I asked myself.

Our good-byes were short, stiff, and self-conscious.

In Joaquin's eyes, I could see him making a decision, which resulted in an awkward hug at my front door and a vague promise to call me.

Trying a joke, I said, "Of course, that's how this all began."

I heard his footsteps taking the outside steps two at a time to the third-floor room. I had told him he might as well stay there now. What difference would one more night make? I closed the front door and wandered through the downstairs, switching on lights to dispel the unexpected anxiety I felt, but they did nothing to erase my increasing apprehension.

"What's not to understand?" I said aloud to the living room walls. Maybe I was naive in the ways of international conspiracies, but I wasn't dumb. "I think I've been insulted," I said to the red lamp with the gold fringe. And I felt my temperature rise.

"He's going off and leaving me to answer to the police, and I'll either have to lie to them again . . . or tell them where he is. How dare he!" I shouted to the four walls, banged my hand on the piano, and shivered again in the loneliness of the house. I was really alone now. The protective aura the house had always provided for me was gone.

Unaccustomed anger seeped into me as I paced and argued with myself. I called out my other half. "Lydia! Lydia, are you going to let him get away with this?"

Lydia!

That name brought back the memory of Steven Miller lying in this room, dying with my alter ego's name on his lips. Mixed with my anger, Steven Miller's unresolved death brought me to a sharp turn in my thinking process.

Who was this Italian-American-quasi-Mexican anyway that he could breeze in and out of countries, in and out of intrigues, in and out of my life, and get away with it? He said he was Arthur Stephen Roselli, but just as someone was coming to prove it, he was skipping the country.

Suddenly I thought I knew. Joaquin wasn't Roselli. Maybe he was one of conspirators who had planned Roselli's death and had been sent to America to tie up any loose ends. Like Bondesky. Sure, and he'd found the perfect chump . . . me . . . to go along with his plans, and then what had happened?

Yes, he'd murdered Steven Miller when Steven had found him searching the house. That's why he'd called out the "Lydia" that Miller had told me about before he died. How stupid I'd been.

I ran to the telephone to call Silas, but stopped before I'd finished dialing the number. I put my finger on the cutoff. Silas wouldn't believe me. Peggy had told me that. But Lennox would! I dialed again, but hung up when the other end answered.

What would I tell him? That Joaquin was skipping out? Certainly. But my other suspicions . . . Would they be enough? I remembered my mistake of accusing Steven Bondesky of Steven Miller's murder.

This time I would make sure before I called in the police.

I didn't call it the war room just because I'd stolen the name from Churchill's underground planning room. I really named it that because that's where the gun lived. It had been there for as long as I could remember. A big one: silver, heavy, and loaded. I'd found it one day when I was very young and all angles and full of curiosity.

My mother had one of her headaches and the usual white cloth was draped over her eyes and forehead. Father had gone for some medication, and I was to watch over Mother, but I could tell she'd drifted off into a light sleep. Bored, I had tiptoed out of the room, into my father's bedroom and—unusual for me—began exploring the knotty-pine drawers and doors built into the wall. In the top of the right-hand one, I'd found the gun.

It looked for all the world like the one Matt Dillon might have carried slung at his side every Saturday night on television . . . one of the few programs Father would let me watch with him.

Fascinated, I'd taken it from the cardboard shoebox and held it in my hand. I'd never felt such strength and power in any object I'd ever touched before. Scared but reluctant to return it to its hiding place, I'd looked around for a safe place to examine it. If Mother woke, she'd come looking for me. I didn't dare take it to my room. How would I get it back to the closet?

I settled on unlocking the screened window in Father's room and sliding under its partial opening to perch on hunkered knees on the small roof overhang outside his room. The gun didn't feel cold or hot to my touch, just big and, oh, so heavy. I turned the barrel toward me and saw the bronze bullets with what I thought were silver tips.

Silver bullets! Then I knew. My father was really the Lone Ranger.

Those thoughts and fantasies occupied my mind for probably a quarter of an hour while sparrows landed beside me, curious as to what the new motionless statue was doing on their roof. It was my mother's plaintive cry of, "Honey, where are you?" that finally brought me from my reverie. I hastened to climb back through the window, stuff the gun into its box, and close the cabinet before she entered the room, the white cloth still clutched to her forehead.

"What have you been doing, Honey?" she asked not in an accusatory tone, but with a genuine desire to know.

"Nothing," I'd said.

I'd never touched the gun again . . . well, only once, after Father died, to verify that it was there.

It still was. As heavy and powerful as I'd remembered it.

My small hand slid around its butt, my finger going naturally to the trigger.

# Thirty-six

I decided to go out the back door. I thought there was less chance of Joaquin hearing that door, protected by the back porch as it was. Putting my hand against the screen, I was startled to see a man standing in the shadows.

"Who . . . ?" I gasped.

"It's all right, Honey. It's me. Ralph." And he stepped into the rectangle of light coming from the back door.

"What are you doing here this late?" I asked, still shaken.

He came closer. "I was working late, and I saw your house blaze up with lights. I thought . . . I thought I might find Joaquin, if we're still allowed to call him that." He laughed.

His attempt at humor went right over my head. "Why?" I asked suspiciously.

"For God's sake, Honey. To give him his check."

And he briefly patted his coat pocket to show where he had it ready.

Then he saw the gun. "What on earth?" He half raised his arms.

"Don't be silly, Ralph," I hissed. I motioned to him, using the gun's long barrel instead of my finger. "Come inside. And be quiet."

"What's all this about?" he asked after he'd followed me into the kitchen.

I decided to trust him. He was here. He'd seen the gun. If I let him leave without an explanation, he'd probably call Silas, and I wasn't ready for that yet.

After I explained my fears, he remained silent, his face white in the bright light of the kitchen, but not from its glare, more like from shock.

Before he'd recovered from my story, I remembered to ask him something that had been bothering me. "Ralph, Silas told me you had checked out Joaquin's references."

"Yes," his voice croaked.

"Well, then, how do you explain why Joaquin is not Joaquin?"

In a stronger tone he answered, "I lied. I wanted someone here to do the garden, and, well . . . hell, Honey, he knew irises."

I gave him a disgusted look as I tried to figure out what to do with the doctor's unexpected visit. "You'll just have to come with me. Yes, that works better, anyway." Even with the gun, I hadn't felt all that secure about confronting Joaquin.

Which is what I planned to do.

Surprisingly, Ralph readily agreed to accompany me.

"Not that I believe you, mind you, but I can't let you go alone, can I?"

We crept up the outside stairs, my pointing out to Ralph the two that creaked and, when we reached the top, I cautiously turned my key at the door.

Joaquin was caught unaware, sprawled across the couch in only his blue jeans, his shirt and coat draped across one of the beanbags, clutching Steven Hyatt's bottle of wine in one hand and a Styrofoam cup in the other.

"What's going on? Honey?" Then, "Ralph!"

Then he saw the gun.

Unlike Ralph, Joaquin's instinct was to dive for the gun, but the bottle and cup in his hands inhibited his attempt, so after one upward lunge, he just settled back in the cushions.

"Does anyone want to tell me what's going on?" he demanded as he set his drink on the floor.

Almost embarrassed, I said, "I think you killed Steven Miller."

"What? Are you crazy?" He looked at Ralph. "What's she saying? Me? Kill Steven Miller?"

Ralph had sidled up beside me, but still within the protection of the weapon, I was having a hard time controlling it in my hand. I moved my left hand up to help support the increasingly heavy object.

"Yes, Joaquin," he answered. "And it occurs to me that she's right."

I flashed him a smile of appreciation for his support. But he went on. "Yes, you killed Steven Miller when you were scouting out the house for the mob or the group that hired you to finish their dirty work."

Although I had told Ralph all my suspicions, he

seemed to be adding to their content, embellishing and elaborating on the original concept. I looked at him, astonished, as I heard him say, "And when Honey found out, she rushed up here to confront you, and you wrestled the gun away from her and shot her."

"What?" I exclaimed, the gun dropping uselessly—barrel down—as I turned to face him, which allowed him to effortlessly take it from me.

"Move over there with Roselli, Honey," he said, using the gun to point the direction.

"I don't understand," I protested as I stumbled toward the couch where Joaquin put his bare arms around me, holding me close. That gesture should have comforted me, but it didn't. We looked up at the man waving the old-fashioned pistol at us.

"What don't you understand, Lydia, honey? Wait a minute, this is even better. First you shoot Joaquin, and then, before he dies, he takes the gun and kills you. That sounds better, doesn't it?"

"No," I answered weakly.

"Ralph," said Joaquin, "this is crazy. You'll never get away with it."

I looked at the man I had trusted, thought I knew so well, and then I understood everything. Too late.

"Lydia?" I repeated Ralph's earlier words. "It was you. You killed Steven Miller. But, why, Ralph? Why? And how did you know about . . . ?" Even with his death threat still ringing in the room, I had to know why.

"About Lydia? From Bondesky, of course. Oh, not directly. Old Jimmy hung around all the time, watching the house for you. That's what he told me. About how he and Bondesky called you by your secret name. How he was protecting you because you didn't know about all that money in the house.'' He laughed.

''I didn't believe him at first. I only questioned him in the beginning because of his always hanging around. I'm surprised you didn't notice him, but then you've always lived here in your own little world, haven't you, Lydia? I envied you that, especially when the big bills for the clinic came due. They took away my Porsche. Did you know that, Lydia?''

Ralph rubbed the end of the gun absently across his nose as he talked. Like he'd forgotten he held it and that this was anything but a social call. ''Linda left me, too.'' He giggled. ''No more money. No more Linda.''

Ralph seemed to remember where he was . . . and why. He turned the gun toward us again, perhaps sensing what I'd felt—Joaquin tensing at my side, preparing to spring.

I eased out of Joaquin's arms to give him more room to maneuver if the chance rose again. ''The money?'' I asked, trying to keep Ralph distracted.

''Yeah, all that money your dad hid in the house for you. You know, I worked late a lot, trying to make things come out all right, but nothing would work. And then, I got to thinking about what Jimmy said.'' He paused. ''We were friends, Jimmy and me. On cold nights, I'd let him sit inside the clinic and watch the house out of the window. Shared my coffee with him. Sometimes, pizza. And he'd talk on and on about his Lydia and the money and how he was going to save her. One night, I just stopped doubting him.''

''But you must have killed him, too?'' I kept on questioning him. Joaquin never said a word, but he sat, coiled on the sofa, ready for Ralph to make a mistake.

''Yeah,'' Ralph said regretfully. ''In the long run, his

loyalty to you ran deeper than his friendship with me. He caught me trying to break in here one day. After Miller's death, Jimmy watched the house every night, and I could only come over in the daytime to search. And Jimmy still caught me. It was probably a good thing, too. I didn't know all those men were hanging around your upstairs. Anyway, Jimmy and I argued in the van. He'd just delivered it and saw me trying to get in one of those big windows off the porch.

"I persuaded him to come back to the van and when he persisted in saying he was going to tell Bondesky, well . . . you know, I shot him. I was surprised no one heard it in the house."

His thoughts brought him back to the present, and I could see that faraway look disappear from his eyes, leaving only a desperate one as he again turned his full attention to the two of us on the couch. I heard Joaquin groan as he realized he'd missed a chance to disarm Ralph.

"Where's the money, Lydia?" Ralph demanded.

"I'll show you," I said, "if you'll let us go."

"No deals. Wait. First I want you to tie up the gardener here." Ralph kept my father's gun pointed toward us as he roamed the room, searching for something to tie us up. Finally, he found a box of black plastic garbage sacks. With scissors from a drawer, he deftly cut the bags into strips while still aiming the gun at us.

I tied Joaquin with the long black strips, first binding his arms behind him as Ralph instructed and then his ankles. When Joaquin was secure—Ralph made sure of that—he put the gun on the couch and reached for me, roughly pulling my arms behind my back. The plastic stretched, but when pulled tight and wrapped repeatedly around my arms, it made a reliable binding. He'd started on my ankles when Joaquin finally spoke.

"Don't tell him where the money is, Honey. He's going to kill us anyway. I'm sorry I couldn't—"

Ralph hit him on the side of the head with my father's big gun.

"We didn't need him anyway," he said, stopping my scream with a threatening motion of the gun. "Now, where's the money?"

I told him.

Or rather, I told him where the money had been. I told him about the secret passage I'd discovered in the blueprints I'd found in the third-floor workroom. How I'd always believed—had even had nightmares—about just such a passageway. I told him about my accidental finding of it and how the money had literally rained down upon my head.

And he believed me. "Yeah, when I saw all those cobwebs in your hair this afternoon, I knew you were up to something. That it would only be a matter of time before you stumbled across the cash. So, where is it—this hiding place?" And he pulled on my trussed arms, hurting my shoulders.

"I'll tell you, but, oh, God, Ralph, please don't kill us."

"Where is the money?"

"There." I nodded my head toward the doorless closet. "Next to that trunk." We both stared at the small, heavy trunk, lying askew just outside the closet. "I found it today. The passageway leads down to the pantry. Under that board. There're not real steps, though. More like an iron ladder. Father must have built it to link the two sections because Aunt Eddie wouldn't have a man in the house at night."

"Shut up. You're crazy, you know that." And he crossed the room in three steps, whereupon, seeing the cut-out section of floorboard, he laid the gun on the trunk and stooped to pry up the already loosened board. "It's dark down there," he said. "And I don't see any money."

"It's farther down," I insisted. "Way down . . . on the first floor. And there's a flashlight that might work in the workroom."

He went to the adjoining workroom and returned with the flashlight, and he grunted when he turned it on and saw that it gave out a dim light, enough to show him his way, but not enough to probe the lower floors for the money.

It had been a tight squeeze for me that afternoon when I'd pushed my way up through the opening. I hadn't wanted to climb down it, so I had prepared the way, rushing upstairs after Joaquin had left for the police station, to push away the trunk and open the trapdoor. That way, when I had returned to the kitchen and started to climb up the metal rungs I'd discovered in the pantry—thanks to the blueprints—I could see daylight above me through the dirt, though most of it had descended on my head earlier when I'd pulled the money through.

I hadn't been afraid, not of the cobwebs or the spiders or the dark. How could I be afraid of something my father had built? Of someplace that he thought secure enough to hide a fortune for me? The nightmares of my youth had vanished when I'd triumphantly completed the secret passage from the first floor to the third and pushed my head through the opening that Ralph was struggling now to enter.

He never gave a backward glance to Joaquin or me; both of us lying tied with our arms behind us. I looked at Joaquin. His eyes were closed, and there was blood trickling from what looked like a nasty knot rising on his forehead. He was either unconscious or dead.

As soon as Ralph's head disappeared from the level of the opening, I began to inch my way toward it. My elbows were immediately scraped and bruised from the rough flooring once I had snaked across the Persian rug, but I kept on, feeling relief when my bound feet finally touched the trunk. I began to push against it with my feet, but it was too heavy for me. Desperately, I leaned against my elbows, pounding the full force of my legs against the sides of the trunk.

I was afraid, but even more than the fear, I was angry. And the more angry I became, the harder I struck the trunk. I started sobbing, "I've never seen the Rose Garden at the White House." I raised my bound legs for another shove. "I've never stood behind Niagara Falls." Then with another push, "Damnit, I want to see my irises bloom."

Below, I heard Ralph cursing, "What the hell? Honey, what are you doing?" And I heard him start upward again. Heard him lose the flashlight, which clanked loudly as it careened past the metal rungs to land with a definite thud on the bottom. Heard Ralph curse again—cruder this time—as he lost a foothold in the darkness and fell. I hoped to the bottom, but it must have been only a few feet, because soon I heard the clanging of his feet as they found another step.

I thought of the Gulf and of the waves that right this

minute were roaring their way toward the shore. I pushed the trunk with all my might. With all I had in me.

And suddenly it slid effortlessly into place. Like it was greased. And then I saw Joaquin's legs next to mine as he gave the final push that sent the trunk squarely over the secret opening.

Without pausing, he raised and twisted his body so that he was lying over the trunk, his head dangling down. ''The other end?'' he gasped.

''Nailed shut. The pantry entry, anyway. I did it this afternoon. And the second floor opening is covered with a big chest of drawers in the war room.'' My breathing pattern matched his, and we sat that way for several minutes, listening to Ralph bang against the bottom of the trunk, calling to me to let him out.

After a while, I inched over to Joaquin, and despite smearing blood all over my white blouse, he managed to bite and tear the plastic rope from my arms. I removed the bindings on my legs and then returned the honor for him, using the scissors Ralph had found to cut the bags.

''So,'' he said when he was finally in an upright position, but still sitting securely on the trunk.

''So,'' I answered, but my thoughts were on Ralph whose pleading had ceased. What must it be like in that dark hole, alone and knowing that everything was coming to an end? I hoped the flashlight was still working. I hoped he had some light.

I walked across the room and bent to pick up the gun from the corner of the room where it had skidded when I'd banged on the trunk.

''Where did you get that antique?'' asked Joaquin. ''And where'd you get the crazy idea that I'd killed

Steven Miller? Or for that matter, that I'm not really Arthur Roselli?''

I stood beside him. ''You were acting so mysterious at dinner. Nervous. All that talk about leaving before the others got here. And then, that strange, strained goodbye.''

Joaquin reached out and pulled me against him, where blood and sweat mingled across his chest. ''Aw, Honey, that was because I do need to get back to Italy. This discovery of mine, the one I thought was going to be so great, is really going to be trouble.''

''It doesn't work,'' I guessed.

He started a frown that ended in a grin. ''No, the trouble is that it does work.''

''I don't understand. No, wait; maybe I do. But you were so distant at dinner tonight. It made me think strange things.''

''I was trying to protect you. To keep you away from what I see ahead. That's why I was trying to avoid this.'' And he kissed me. And I kissed him back. He pulled away and said, ''Just think if I'd done this in the first place, we'd never have all the fun we've had tonight.''

# Thirty-seven

Options.

For a person who lived every day with a typewritten plan, I had lots of options.

Steven Hyatt wanted me to go to Australia with him. "As my primary—oh, all right, my only investor—I'd think you would want to see how I'm spending your money. And how I'm going make us more. I'm really on to something hot here, Honey. Won't you come with me?"

And Harry. I knew I loved Harry, but was it only on the island? Or was it the dog? I couldn't separate the two. If I loved Harry so much, how come I'd felt the way I did about Joaquin?

Joaquin. Arthur Stephen Roselli. For sure. The man who hadn't been able to slip back across the border after all, because he'd had to wait for the police to guide a dazed, light-blinded Ralph from the concealed passageway in my house.

"Where's the money, Honey?" Ralph had screamed

when he could finally focus his eyes and saw me standing there with Silas Sampson.

"What's he talking about? Money?" asked Silas.

And because it was Silas and he was so easy to lie to, I said, "I don't know what he's talking about, Silas. There's no money. See for yourself."

I was glad it was Silas and not Lennox who'd asked.

Ralph had gone berserk then, yelling and raving about Jimmy and Steven Miller. Even ripping open his starched white shirt to show the almost healed wound Steven Miller's big flashlight had made when the poor man had struck him, right before Ralph shot him.

Joaquin had stayed and met the authorities from Italy, and it was big news in the *Star-Telegram* about him being alive. And about his discovery. Like Bondesky had said, all kinds began crawling out of the woodwork, and we'd had little time together. But it had been good. When he left—just this morning—just three weeks after the first telephone call, he asked me to come with him. Or even later. I could come later.

He was definitely an option.

Janie Bridges had squealed when I called to tell her the news. I wanted her to hear it from me before it hit the airwaves. "I told you it was Ralph," she said.

"Janie," I said, "you didn't."

"I'm sure I did. Well, if I didn't, I should have. Remember I said the killer would be at the funeral. And, Honey, Ralph was at the funeral. And next time . . . next time I'll get it all right."

Anyway, it was late Saturday evening when I was finally alone in my house again. I'd driven Joaquin—he'd always be Joaquin to me—to the airport. The Plymouth Voyager was really a dream to drive. I wondered what it would do on the open road.

Work was my final option. I could keep on doing what I was doing. I enjoyed it, and Bondesky insisted he could still keep up with my records from jail. And he might not be there so very long, anyway.

No, I suddenly thought, work wasn't my final option after all. There was the money. And the house.

I'd have to move the money. I knew that. But right now, I felt it was safe in the piano. After all, it lay in the passageway above the pantry for over seventeen years. Almost as long as the toys under the house. I wondered then if Father had known about the moldy box of contraband I'd left under the back porch. Wondered if that was where he'd gotten the idea to hide the money within the house?

I really didn't have to work again—ever.

I could stay home and watch over the house. As it had always watched over me.

No, I could put a name to my guardian angel now: Jimmy. The odious man whom I'd so visibly shunned. I was the one who knew that you didn't judge a book by its cover, and I'd done just that with Jimmy, allowing my obvious revulsion of the derelict to cloud any positive premonitions that he might have emitted. I remembered his puppy-dog eagerness to assist me at Bondesky's command, and I shrugged. How was I to know? But I knew now, and my house had lost the breathing, watchful presence, which had never really been the house at all.

Maybe I couldn't trust my feelings after all. Again I wondered. What option would Aunt Eddie approve of?

I carried my guilt upstairs with me as heavily as I did

the large package that had arrived in the mail from one of the publishing houses I represented. It contained samples of a new line of computer manuals they were starting to carry. Dutifully, I lugged them up into the war room to record the shipment, then I decided idly to check what was supposed to be my itinerary for next week.

Palo Pinto! Sweetwater! Odessa! How could I have forgotten that west Texas was next on my schedule? I had planned to try out a little ranch-looking motel outside Abilene this time. What was its name? I looked through the west Texas files. I hated not remembering. I didn't find the motel name on my first immersion into the files, but I did pull out a large manila envelope, and I smiled when I remembered where I'd picked it up.

There was this little bookseller in Breckenridge who had taken me to a barbecue joint for lunch. Over chopped beef sandwiches and tall glasses of iced tea, he'd shyly thrust the envelope into my hands.

"It's a book I've written," he said. "I'd appreciate it . . . consider it an honor . . . if you'd take a look at it. Tell me what you think of it."

I had pulled the neatly stacked pages from their cover as he continued to talk about his work. "It's not much, really. I mean, I think it's a real book, but then again, I don't know. Is it too much to ask, Honey? For you to read it? It's only a little made-up story. You don't have to. . . ."

This had happened to me before. Booksellers were book-lovers—well, all except Harry—and most were frustrated writers. I had meant to take the manuscript to Boston with me. To read it at night so I would be prepared when I saw the little man again. I always hated having to tell them if I didn't like the book. I sighed and looked at my watch. It wasn't all that late, and if I did decide to go . . .

Taking the book downstairs with me, I lighted what was probably going to be the last fire of the season. As the gas flames cast their dancing shadows on the hearth, their capricious frolic the only spirits left in the house, I curled up before the fire and turned to the first page.

Before I began to read, I remembered what I had replied to the would-be author. "I'd be glad to read it. Who knows? It might be a best-seller. And besides, there's always room in the world for another good story."

And part of what I told him was true.

If you enjoyed *The Fourth Steven*, then read the following excerpt from

# Grinning in His Mashed Potatoes

the next Honey Huckleberry mystery.

*Coming to your bookstore in 1999.*

The second bestselling author in the world ate his dessert first.

I probably wouldn't have noticed, but I was sitting next to him, and when he took that first bite of the Eagle Brand lemon pie with the mile-high meringue, I wished I had the nerve to do the same.

My mother always said, "Eat your vegetables first." So I did, even though she died more than ten years ago. She might have had a point. Twyman Towerie licked the meringue off his lips with a satisfied grin and fell over dead into his mashed potatoes.

And I lived to tell the tale.

Of course, there was a scream. And, of course, it came from my friend Janie who was also sitting at the squared head table at the Arlington Friends of the Library Annual luncheon. Although she is a devoted mystery fan and reads blood and gore without batting a lash, Janie always screams when she sees a dead body. She's working on it, but Towerie's death made her two for two.

Association with death—murder—to be exact is why Janie and I wound up at the head table usually reserved for authors and their friends. I was recently featured in the *Fort Worth Star-Telegram* as having had two—not one, but two—murders occur in my life. And since I am a book representative for a small, respectable number of publishers, the Friends of the Arlington Public Library naturally assumed that the combination of books, murder, and publicity would help entice more readers to their fund-raiser.

Janie accepted the invitation for me and had announced to the chairman over the phone that she would be my lunch partner. She's into books too, owns a coverted gas station in West Texas that sells all kinds of paperbacks, but specializes in mysteries.

Although romances, not mysteries, were my thing, I was actually getting quite good at knowing what to do when one finds a corpse. Or in this case, sitting next to one.

After my first embarrassed reaction—"Mr. Towerie . . . are you all right?"—I realized he was not and jumped to my feet. Not used to wearing high heels, I had slipped them off under the table. Now my left foot scrambled to find a toehold on the missing shoe while my right one slipped into a slot between the straps. I made an uneven lurch toward the downed author.

I put my hand on his shoulder and the big gray head rolled off his plate onto the table. That was about as far as my expertise went and I looked out into the audience and said the numbers that had helped me before. "911! 911!"

The faces that seemed frozen for the few seconds since the previous action had taken place suddenly went into overdrive, creating a blurred image of a previously still picture. A few darted off to the hallway, hopefully to call the magic number, and two purposeful bodies headed toward Twyman.

"Doctor."

"Doctor."

I assumed that meant they were doctors, so I stepped aside to let them at him. Of course, that was another lurch, which threw me back into my chair so I got to see all the resuscitation stuff up close. The two—a man and a woman—gently laid Twyman on the floor, loosening his tie and belt while opening his shirt. I looked away then, but could hear the pounding swooshing sounds that obviously went with the correct professional behavior in such a situation. After several minutes, they both shouted, "911! 911!"

Slowly slipping sideways, chair by chair, I managed to take myself out of the center of the action. By the time the emergency crew arrived I had nearly made it to the other side of the table. I couldn't see what they were doing to Twyman, but their actions certainly seemed competent. The room, which had produced a varied cacophony of sounds following the initial realization of stunned silence, now was quiet as a tomb again. Janie stood behind me, her strong fingers digging into my shoulder.

Finally the EMTs looked at each other and the attending physicians and shook their heads. "Let's get him to the hospital," one said. Although it was evident even to me that the morgue was the obvious destination. None of the professionals would take the responsibility of declaring Twyman deceased, but I heard the woman doctor whisper "as a doornail" to the luncheon's chairperson, Elaine Madison. And down Texas way, doornails are always dead.

NOW AVAILABLE IN HARDCOVER
DANA STABENOW
KILLING GROUNDS
PUTNAM